All rights reserved, no part of this publication
may be either reproduced or transmitted
by any means whatsoever without the prior
permission of the publisher
VENEFICIA PUBLICATIONS UK
veneficiapublications.com
veneficiapublications@gmail.com
Typesetting © Veneficia Publications
UK September 2021

Text © Scott Irvine
All images are from Scott Irvine and the public
domain, and were modified for cover by Diane
Narraway
Edited by Veneficia Publications, with
additional editing by Fi Woods.

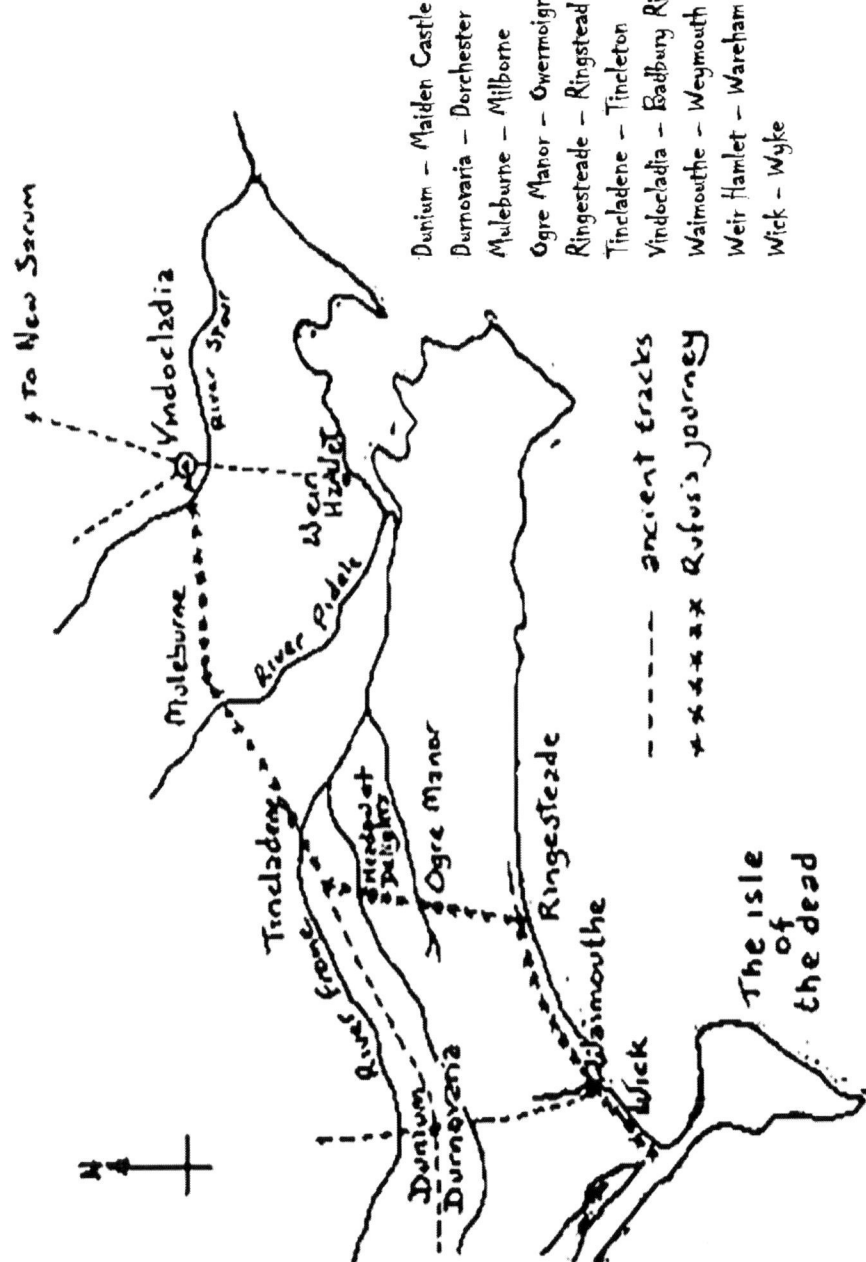

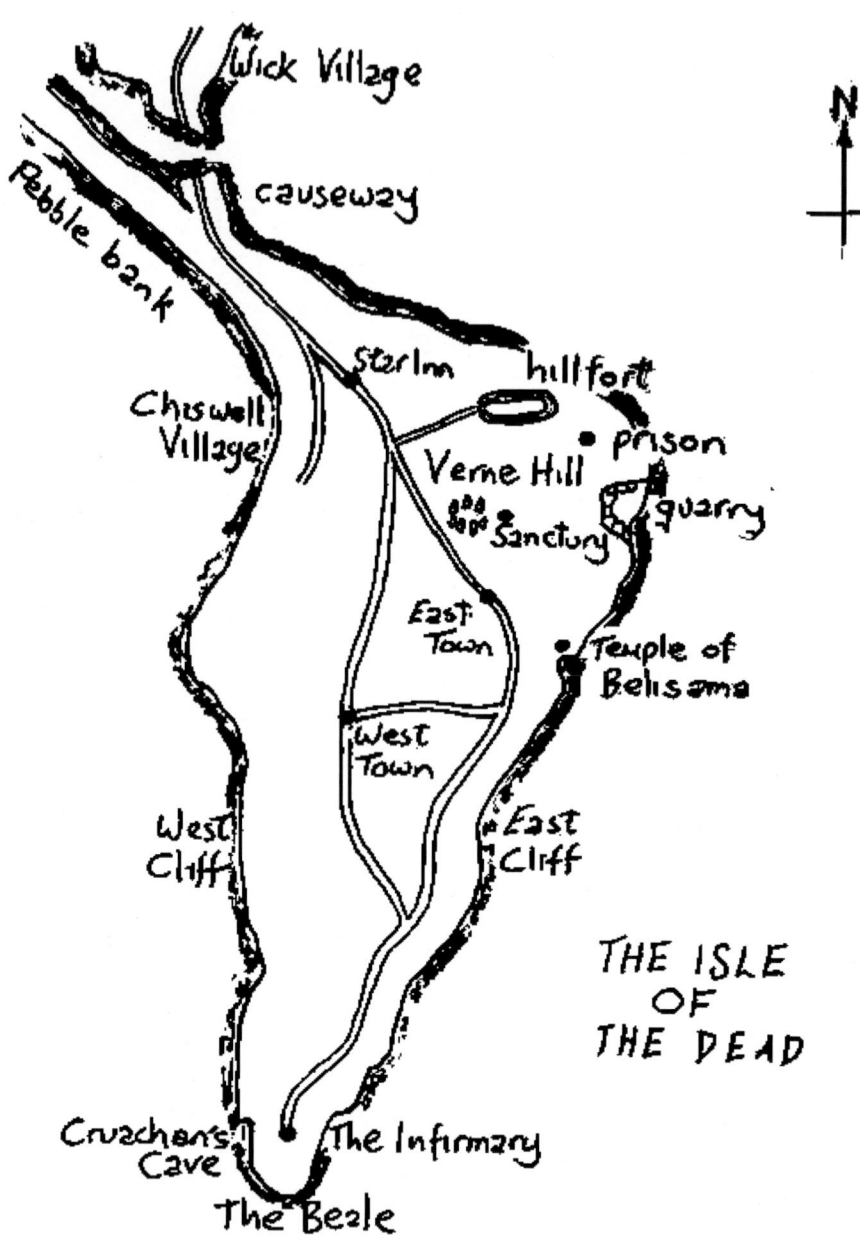

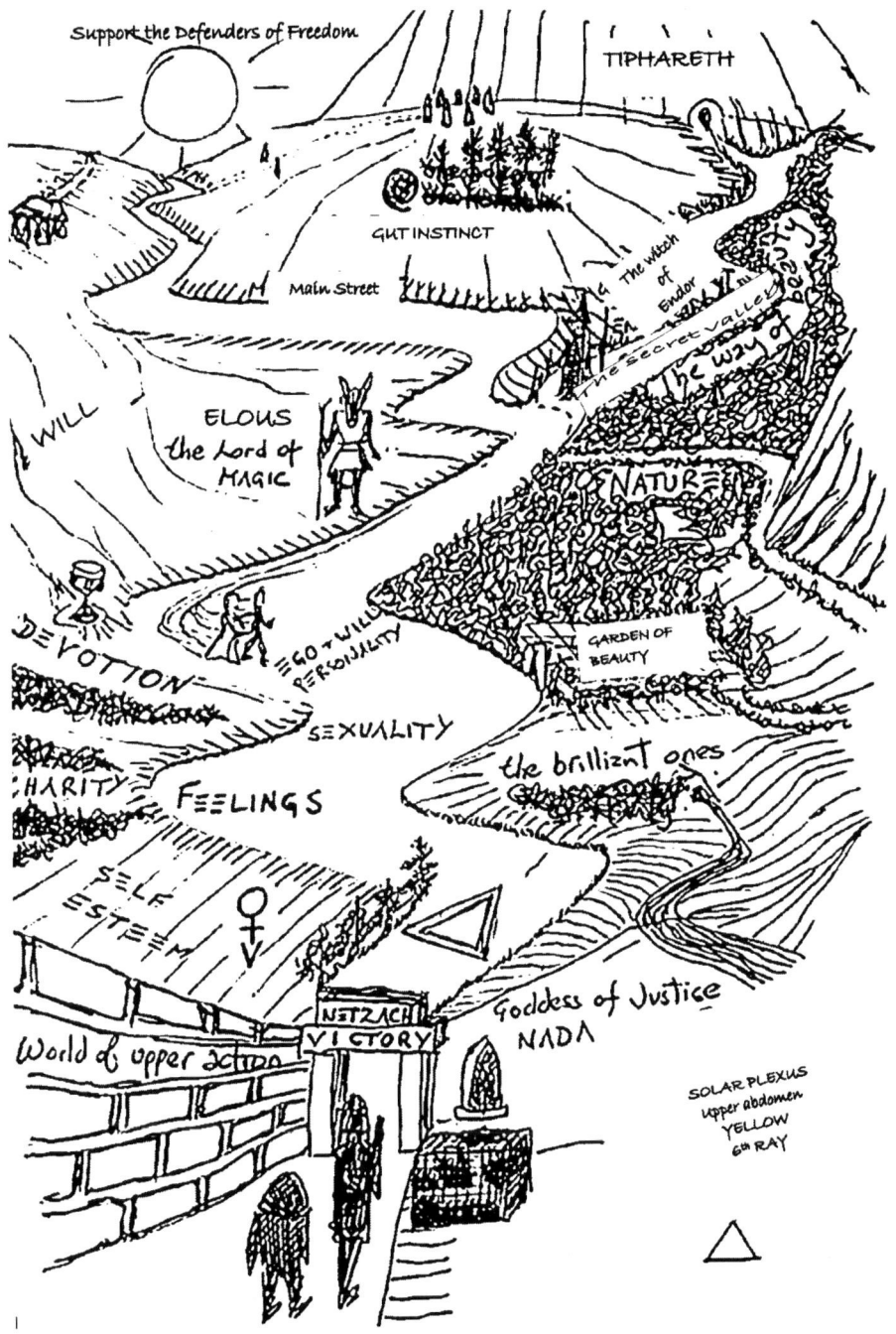

THE KING'S ODYSSEY

by

Scott Irvine

The King's Odyssey

The Oracle	1
The Meadow of Delights	11
Ogre Manor	20
The Island of the Dead	30
Crossing the Causeway	42
Hard Labour	54
Swan Feather	67
Moon Magic	80
Transformation	90
A Man Again	101
To the Beale	109
Into the Underworld	122
Cruachan's Cave	133
Eoaster Greetings	144
Dead Cats Don't Meow	158
All the King's Men	170
Good Vibrations	180
Astral Adventure	192
Battle Stations	203
Battle of Portland	213

*An ancient adventure of heroes and magic,
of witches and druids, and of love, seduction,
and heartbreak*

THE ORACLE

Allow me to tell you a tale of travel and adventure. It is the story of an ancestor of mine from long ago. His name was King Rufus and he ruled over the Kingdom of Vindocladia in the realm of Wessex, in the south of the island of Albion. This was at a time when the Gods and Goddesses were still revered and honoured by the people. Dragons ruled the skies, hobgoblins roamed in the deep forests, and sea nymphs lured men to a watery death. It was a time when faeries gathered at rivers and springs, and magic and spells were still being cast. Men followed the code of chivalry and women were ladies. It was a very long time ago.

Before dawn had a chance to paint the eastern sky with red and the morning songs of the birds began, a solitary figure slipped out of the castle unseen. The man walked confidently the hill to the sleeping village that surrounded the castle. The man wore a simple green cloak, not too flash nor too shabby. The hood covered his face as he quietly made his way through the village. He carried with him his trusty staff of holly. The man owned three staffs: an oak staff for its hardness that he used for fighting, a willow staff for its softness that he used for walking, and the one he had with him today. The holly staff was best for general use: it was ideal for both fighting and walking. It was his favourite staff and he had named it Caliburn.

The man reached the edge of the village before turning back towards the castle for a final glance. It was his castle, for he was the King. King Rufus was his name, and he was starting out on an adventure that had been recommended by his prophet after reading the entrails of a goat.

'King Rufus, my Lord,' the prophet had declared, 'the omens are telling me that you must go in search of a magical realm outside your kingdom. You must journey alone and in secret after the great Festivals of Beltane have finished.'

The King had heeded his prophet's advice. The Beltane fires had burnt themselves out a week ago and the Stag Lord, the King of Nature, had descended into the world of man bringing with him the fresh spirit of nature. Leaves were starting to appear on the trees and flowers were starting to bloom. Cattle were being released into fields after the dark winter months. The land was coming alive once more. The King loved this time of year. It was a good time for a quest. He turned his back on his castle and the village. However, before stepping into the thick, darkness of the ancient forest that separated all the Kingdoms, he asked the Mother Goddess for guidance and protection.

Shafts of morning sun penetrated the forest as the King walked the well-defined path that headed towards the small hamlet of Muleburne, 10 miles east of his castle at Vindocladia.

Vindocladia was the meeting place of three major roads that connected his empire to New Sarum in the north, and the great stone temple beyond, Werham to the south by the Great Pool, and the town of Durnovana to the east in the shadow of the great castle of Dunium. The King's prophet had told him to go in search of a magical realm, but he could not tell him where to find this land; however, he knew someone who could. Near to the hamlet of Muleburn lived the Oracle, Nimue, a priestess of beauty and wisdom. The King had used the Oracle several times in the past, and she had always proved to be correct in her prophecies. It was one of these prophecies that had led to him meeting his wife, princess Carolyn; the daughter of King Dalan and Queen Calatin, whose kingdom lay in the mountains of Gymry far out to the west.

Along with his staff, the King had brought a shoulder bag containing a purse of silver coins, a roll of twine, and some dried meat and bread the housemaid had prepared for him the night before., and He also carried a dagger that was fashioned by the mystical hands of the faerie folk. It was said that the blade would cut through any material and kill any demon or unearthly creature it stabbed. This magical blade, Rufus kept hidden in one of his sturdy leather boots.

    The sun was high in the sky when the King neared Muleburn, as he sat by the River Pidele to rest and have a snack before visiting the Oracle. He found himself a spot under an old oak and ate a little of his bread and meat. While eating, the King thought back to the time of his first ever meeting with the Oracle, when he was still a young prince. His father, King Angus, had been away for some time fighting in the Brecon Hills of Gymry. He was helping one of his allies King Dalan to defend his Kingdom from Northern Pict invaders Things were not going well, and the King had sent a message for Prince Rufus to help the cause. The prince had a personal army of a hundred soldiers which he kept fighting fit, but Rufus did not agree with violence of any kind and had always been able to steer clear of warfare. King Angus had sent the young prince away at an early age, to New Sarum, to train in the art of fighting. Rufus preferred the staff over the sword, axe, bow, and spear to defend himself, as it was less likely to kill anyone. He was quite happy to crack a skull or two and break a man's balls, leaving the killing to his troops. In fact, Rufus so enjoyed the feel of the staff that he practiced with it every day, even when his training had finished. Rufus considered himself to be the best staff fighter in the whole Kingdom of

Wessex. He became so confident that he would command one of his troops to fire an arrow at him to catch in the wood of the staff. One day though, probably after too much wine, he tried to defend himself from two arrows, misjudged the flights, and was struck by one of the arrows in his right thigh. It hurt. The scar still remains to this day and reminds him of the incident when it niggles in cold conditions.

Anyway, as I have already mentioned, the prince had reservations about fighting wars that he considered none of his business, but at the same time he had a duty to his father. Rufus had heard about the Oracle and decided it was time to call on her for advice. Nimue readily welcomed the prince; she told him that going to help his father would set him up in good stead as the future king, and at the same time he would find the love of his life. On this advice, the prince took his army to Gymry and helped his father and King Dalan repel the invaders. In doing so, he won the respect of his father and King, and won the hand of Dalan's eldest daughter: Princess Carolyn.

A rustle in the bushes broke his thoughts and Rufus automatically reached for Caliburn. He looked around for its source but could see nothing although he felt someone, or something, was watching him. The King decided it was time to move on and took a drink from the river before leaving. It was time to meet the Oracle.

Heading north upriver towards the Oracle's temple, the King still felt that eyes were watching him from the undergrowth. He held his trusty staff close to his chest ready for an ambush. Suddenly, up ahead on the path a warrior appeared, dressed in leather armour, and carrying a short sword. Rufus found a good footing and held Caliburn ready to resist an attack. The warrior stood motionless, seemingly unconcerned at the King's presence. Then, a beautiful woman wearing a gown of morning mist appeared from the same place as the warrior, stood by him, and held her hand out towards the King.

'Rufus my friend, I have been expecting you,' the woman spoke in a gentle voice. 'Don't mind the warrior, he is employed by me to guard against attacks from the hobgoblins.' The King recognized her as the Oracle Nimue. 'Times are changing fast,' she continued, 'I see a new god in my visions, sweeping all other gods and goddesses before him like a dark cloud from the east.'

He lowered his weapon and greeted the priestess with a kiss on the cheek. Nimue went on to tell the King about recent incursions of the hobgoblins around Muleburne and the surrounding areas, attacking the villagers and stealing food and cattle. The Oracle believed that a higher force was controlling the normally secretive creatures, making them behave in ways that stirred up the lives of mankind, but she could not think why.

'I need your help to seek a magical realm outside my kingdom,' the King told the Oracle.

Nimue walked back to her camp with Rufus, along a path through dense undergrowth.

'I am sorry I have not yet been able to find out who abducted your son or why he was taken,' spoke Nimue, as they entered the camp, which was encircled by standing stones. 'I have been led to believe he is across the water in Armorica, being cared for by the faeries,' she continued.

Armorica thought the King, the land of the Bretons; he knew it well. I bet Morgan le Fay was behind it, contemplated the King.

The King had spent some time in Armorica as a prince, studying the Art of War with a master from the east called Sun Tzu, and swordsmanship with the samurai Miyamato Musashi. These studies took place at Penpon, in the centre of the Enchanted Forest of Broceliande that covered most of the region of Armorica. It was here that he met Morgan le Fay, a beautiful faerie, but not one to be trusted. As beautiful and charming as the faerie was, the young prince was in love with his Gymrian princess and refused her advances, until she entranced him into making love to her in her cave. She tried to keep him prisoner for his unfaithfulness to his betrothed Carolyn but, because she tricked him, he refused to stay with her and threatened to cut her head off unless she released him. Reluctantly, she let Rufus go, but swore she would get her own back.

She has taken my heir as revenge, thought the King.

Nimue had read his thoughts and told him not to jump to conclusions. She would find out for sure where his son was being held and inform him in due course. The King struggled to put the matter to the back of his mind as the pair made their way to a stone temple at the centre of the camp.

A young priestess came from a tent and motioned for the King to sit in a chair, before returning with a goblet of wine for him while Nimue prepared herself to talk to the gods. A fissure in the ground emitted vapours that induced an ecstasy in the Oracle as she sat on a golden tripod As the King watched and enjoyed his wine, Nimue started to utter strange words: the tongue of the angels. The sun was now at its zenith in the clear sky above the clearing that held the Oracle's temple. Nimue seemed to ride on waves of emotions, one minute excited and poetic and the next, groaning and twisting her body as if in agony. Soon she was done and the young priestess who had served the King helped the exhausted Oracle from her golden stool and ushered her into the tent behind the King. He was deep in thought; the sight of the Oracle in action never ceased to amaze him every time he visited. It was a spectacular experience to see.

Shortly afterwards, the young priestess exited the tent and came to stand facing Rufus. It was she, who interpreted the words of the Oracle. The King finished his wine and put the goblet on the small table beside his chair. 'The Oracle has spoken to the gods through the mediation of the angels,' the priestess told the King. 'This is the response the gods gave to your question regarding the location of the mystical land you seek,' Rufus sat up in his chair. "Southern voices calling to you, mystic magic, and seas of blue. Timeless marvels cease to wonder when you know the spell, you're under. Secret sounds of giant sea birds, singing songs of a lonesome end. Golden cats in temples of stone, the spells of time are your friend."

The King was a little surprised at the interpretation; it was not what he was expecting.

Timeless marvels? Golden cats in temples? This was no help.

'It does not really tell me where I will find this mystical land,' protested the King, 'I do not understand its meaning.'

'I can only relate what the Oracle spoke,' asserted the priestess. 'It is up to you to make of it what you will.'

Rufus scratched his head. He knew the priestess was telling the truth and could assist him no more. Rising from his seat he thanked the priestess, took a silver coin from his purse, and placed it in a bowl next to the tent. The priestess smiled at the King, and he kissed her on the cheek before making his way out of the temple site. He nodded to the warrior as he continued his journey westwards towards Tincladene and a bed before sundown.

THE MEADOW OF DELIGHTS

The riddle the Oracle had given the King was going around in his mind as he made his way towards the small hamlet of Tincladene. He needed to reach the valley of small farms before nightfall; he did not fancy being out in the forest for the night. He much preferred the comfort and protection of a room to a cold and foreboding forest. The King was aware of eyes following him as he walked but decided that whatever was watching him posed no immediate threat.

The King reached Tincladene, which sat on the banks of the Fair River, as the orange ball of the sun set upon on the horizon. Amongst the small farms that made up the village of Tincladene, Rufus found accommodation at the Sun Inn, which backed onto the river. Before settling down for the night, the King enjoyed a tankard of ale in the bar. He sat at a table near to the door, contemplating the riddle that the Oracle had given him, when he was joined by a thin man dressed in an expensive red suit of clothes.

'Mind if I join you, good sir?' the skinny man asked, as he sat opposite Rufus. 'My name is Lord Belvedore,' the man continued. He placed a large ewer of ale on the table between them and topped up the King's tankard. Rufus thanked the well-dressed stranger and told him that his name was Rufus, from Vindocladia. He told Lord Belvedore that he was a carpenter on his way to Durnovaria to do some work in the castle. He kept the fact that he was a King secret. He could do without the intrusion of the skinny man but felt obliged to be polite.

'How can I help you?' asked Rufus.

'It is I that can help you,' replied Lord Belvedore, as he pulled from his bag a collection of fur things.

'The best coney fur in the land,' the stranger continued, 'Hats, gloves, boots, whatever you fancy at a knock-down price!' Rufus looked at the man's merchandise, then up at him.

'I do not need any of that, thank you sir,' replied Rufus, taking a generous mouthful of ale. Lord Belvedore topped up the tankard once again.

'How about a lucky coney paw?' he continued.

'No thank you,' insisted Rufus, starting to get irritated with the intrusion but Lord Belvedore had not finished yet, much to the annoyance of Rufus.

'I can get you anything you want,' the stranger persisted, 'Women? Boys? Tell me what you want, and I guarantee that I can get it,' insisted Lord Belvedore.

'Anything?' enquired Rufus.

'I guarantee it,' boasted the man in red.

'I am looking for a magical realm,' explained Rufus, taking another large swig of his ale. 'In the south by the sea,' he continued, unsure of how much he should reveal to the stranger. Lord Belvedore thought for a second, rubbing his large, pointed chin.

'I know of a place,' whispered Lord Belvedore 'A place called The Meadow of Delights, about five miles south of here, a beautiful magic clearing in the forest beside a river.'

'Five miles south from here, you say?' asked Rufus, beginning to take an interest in the stranger. It could not do any harm in visiting, he decided. 'How much for you to take me there?' enquired the cautious traveller.

'You, my friend, I will take for nothing. I have to go that way tomorrow anyhow,' insisted Lord Belvedore. 'I will be leaving early: as soon as the sun rises. Meet me outside here and we will travel together to the Meadow of Delights.'

With that, the strange man in the red suit saluted to Rufus, bidding him farewell, gathered up his furs, and left the tavern as quickly as he had arrived. He had left behind the ewer of ale on the table.

Waste not want not, thought Rufus, and spent the rest of the evening finishing the ale. The bar had filled up with locals who were merrily drinking and singing the night away.

As dawn painted the morning sky red, orange, and yellow, Rufus stood outside the

Sun Inn waiting for Lord Belvedore to arrive. A cool breeze wrapped itself around the king as he looked up and down the street. The village was empty of souls this early in the morning. Then a lone figure walking towards him, silhouetted against the morning sunrise, caught his eye. It was the stranger in red, with his sack of furs over his shoulder, a black brimmed hat shielding his face, and a sword tucked into his belt.

'Good morning, Rufus, my friend,' called Lord Belvedore. The king gave a wave of his hand towards the man and waited for him to reach him before returning conversation.

'Good morning to you, sir. I am ready for you to show me the Meadow of Delights you promised last night.'

Lord Belvedore smiled at the king, 'Of course my friend, follow me. We shall reach the place in an hour or so.' The King took up his staff and walked alongside Lord Belvedore out of Tincladene, with the rising sun behind them, and took the path through the forest leading towards the great town of Durnovaria.

The pair followed the river for a time before coming to a bridge that led to another path through the forest, heading south.

'This is the path to the Meadow of Delights,' said Lord Belvedore, pointing towards the old wooden bridge that straddled the river.

Beams of sunlight darted in through the canopy of leaves as the sun continued to rise overhead. The forest was much denser south of the river and the path more constricted, and much less travelled. The squeals of animals could be heard in the distance. Rufus took a firm grip of his trusty staff, Caliburn, before taking the lead over the bridge and into the dark woods on the other side. The King could feel the same eyes looking at him that he sensed on his way to the Oracle the day before.

'These woods are foreboding,' Rufus thought out loud.

'Nonsense,' replied Lord Belvedore, 'I come up and down this way regularly and have witnessed nothing more than a scared deer and a few long-eared conies, bobbing about in the undergrowth from time to time.' He gave Rufus a reassuring pat on the back, took the lead along the path, and began to whistle a tune as he walked. Rufus was not reassured but could not show his discomfort; after all, he was a brave king. He followed on behind the strange man in red, staying alert to everything around him. The forest was too dense to see very far and for all the King knew a monster could be only feet away, ready to strike.

But Rufus needn't have worried; they shortly arrived at a large clearing, which seemed extremely bright after the darkness of the forest. A large standing stone dominated the area and a stream flowed across the expanse. It looked very serene and immediately Rufus began to relax.

'Welcome to the Meadow of Delights,' announced Lord Belvedore, as he gestured with his hand at the scene before them. The meadow was awash with colour: red poppies, pink of peonies, yellow dahlias, and pale blue foxgloves. It was truly a meadow of delights, such as the king had never seen.

'Let us rest for a while by the standing stone,' announced the mysterious man in red.

'I have brought food and drink.' Lord Belvedore continued.

'And then I will leave you to search for what you are looking for in peace and continue on my way with a full stomach and a quenched thirst,' stressed Lord Belvedore, as he sat by the large standing stone and began removing some of the contents from his bag. Rufus, now fully at ease, joined him beside the nine-foot, grey, limestone megalith. Lord Belvedore offered a slab of cheese and a crust of bread, and Rufus thanked him before eagerly devouring the food. While he ate, Rufus took in the surrounding scenery and enjoyed the view. A few clouds in the heavens obscured the sun now and again, creating shadows that raced across the meadow. Birdsong accompanied the rippling of the small stream that flowed eastwards in front of the two men. A cool breeze rustled the leaves in the forest surrounding them; this is paradise indeed, thought Rufus.

After the pair had eaten, Lord Belvedore passed a goatskin of wine to Rufus, who drank the sweet contents gladly and thanked the stranger for his kindness once again. Lord Belvedore smiled as he watched his companion relax and stretch in satisfaction. The king felt good in himself, and his eyes grew heavy as he relaxed against the great stone, his mind beginning to wander. What was the riddle the Oracle had given him? Southern voices calling to you,

Mystic magic seas of blue, Timeless marvels ... Rufus could not remember of the rest.

What did this place have to do with the riddle? What did this place have to do with anything?

Rufus tried to open his eyes, but a deep tiredness had gripped him. He felt comfortably numb as the pleasantness of the warm sun caressed his weary body. He failed to notice the man in red remove a length of cord from his bag and reach over towards him.

When Rufus came around, his head was spinning, and he felt sick. Worse still, he found himself tethered by his wrists to the standing stone behind him.

What was going on?

As his mind cleared, he realised that the stranger had deceived him, but for what purpose? He could see the contents of his bag on the ground in front of him, minus the coins, and his staff some distance away, lying in the grass. Rufus could feel the trusty "Fireblade," his dagger made by the faeries, still safely hidden inside his boot and was glad that he took the precaution to conceal it there that morning. Unfortunately, he could not reach the weapon to free himself; he was helpless until somebody came along to free him. He did not have to wait long. Coming out of the forest from the southern edge of the meadow, the King saw several figures striding towards him. At first, he could not make out their features, but as they waded across the river, he could see that they were hobgoblins, heavily armed with swords and clubs and making their way straight towards him.

The smell of the hideous creatures reached Rufus about a minute before they were standing at his feet, sneering, and prodding him with their weapons.

'Another poor sap for the Ogre,' observed the fattest and most disgusting hobgoblin.

'Lorac will be pleased,' replied another, 'this one at least has some meat on his bones,' he continued. The group of hobgoblins laughed at this comment.

'Will be worth several gold pieces I think,' continued the first creature, rubbing his dirty hands in glee, which caused another outburst of laughter from the group.

Rufus stared at the motley crew of fat, slimy, swine in front of him, as he slowly regained his composure. He knew from experience that these creatures were not the most intelligent of beings and once he was free would be able to make his escape. He decided to play along to find out what they were up to.

'What do you want with me?' pleaded Rufus. 'Please don't hurt me.' The leader of the group spat out a great green globule of slime that landed on the ground beside the king before replying.

'Oh, it's not what we are going to do with you that you have to worry about my friend, but what the ogre is going to do with you.' The chief hobgoblin called to a comrade to untie the prisoner, while the others kept their swords aimed at the king. Once free, Rufus stood, rubbing his sore wrists where the cord had been tied. He was a good two feet taller than his captors and they looked up at him warily as he gazed around the clearing, his mind working out a way to escape as the hobgoblins forced him back towards the way they had come.

OGRE MANOR

The sun had passed its zenith in the heavens as Rufus rose to his feet surrounded by the hobgoblins. His mind was already hatching a plan of escape, but for the time being he was going to play along with his captors to find out what their game was. After looking through the contents of his bag the hobgoblins ordered the king to go with them. Rufus put his plan into immediate effect and screamed in pain as he put his weight onto his left leg. His captors stared at him.

'I have an injured leg,' Rufus protested, 'I need my staff to walk with.' The leader of the hobgoblins stared at Rufus with suspicion before grunting.

'Do you think I am stupid? The staff is a weapon you will use against us.'

'No, it is a crutch to aid my walking. I twisted my ankle in the woods on the way here.' Rufus countered. The leader waved away his protest and pushed Rufus forward, towards the southern edge of the meadow. Rufus fell to the ground, clutching his leg.

'Get up,' screamed the leader, 'Before I hit you with your own staff.' Rufus stood up slowly and put on a convincing limp, moving at a snail's pace in the direction of the woods.

'We will never get to Ogre Manor at this rate,' complained one of the hobgoblins, and shoved Rufus in the back in an attempt to hurry him up. Rufus fell to the ground once more.

'I need my staff,' pleaded Rufus, as he lifted himself from the floor. 'There are seven of you and I am not a warrior, only a simple carpenter. How can I possibly defeat seven mighty hobgoblins on my own and with an injured leg?' The hobgoblins mumbled amongst themselves for a bit, deciding what to do.

'We could carry him,' suggested one of them.

'No, let's march him at knife-point; he will get a move on then.' grunted another. The debate went on for several minutes before the leader raised his hands, asking for quiet.

'He is only a man and men are weak,' the leader growled, 'even with his staff he cannot overpower us. Give him his staff or we will never get to Ogre Manor before nightfall.' There were a few snorts and grunts among the captors before the staff was reluctantly returned to the king.

Rufus took the staff and followed the hobgoblins over the river and into the woods.

'What business do you have with Lord Belvedore?' Rufus enquired to the hobgoblin walking beside him.

'Who?' came the reply.

"The man who brought me to you, leaving me tied to the sarsen stone in the meadow,' replied Rufus. The hobgoblin scratched his chin as he thought,

'Oh, you mean Red Jack,' he retorted.

'Sounds like the man,' said Rufus, 'Who is this Red Jack and what is your business with him?' The hobgoblin stared at Rufus.

'Red Jack comes from the Island of the Dead across the bay and brings us fools like you for Lorac, the ogre, to ransom back to your people.'

'What is in it for you?' enquired Rufus. Before the hobgoblin could reply, he was whipped about the head with the hand of his leader.

'Shut up you moron,' barked the leader, 'tell the man nothing. No more talking. He is our prisoner and the less he knows the better.'

The group moved south through the forest towards Ogre Manor. Rufus was aware of the stillness that surrounded him: no birds or animals moved. Apart from snorts and the occasional fart from his captors, Rufus sensed that life in the forest was dead, or at least silent, for a reason.

They had travelled for over an hour in silence when they came out of the forest into a large opening; in the distance stood a large manor house. The building had seen better days; even from a distance Rufus could see its dilapidated state. Fit for an ogre, he thought.

The group stopped. The leader of the hobgoblins turned and looked at Rufus.

'I thought it was your left leg that you hurt,' he growled. Rufus glared at the creature, then looked down at his leg before glancing around at the rest of the group.

'No, it was my right leg,' Rufus insisted.

'Liar,' screamed the chief, 'it was your left leg you were limping on when we left the meadow and now you are limping on your right! You have been deceiving us.' Rufus realised his mistake, concluding the hobgoblin leader was not as stupid as he looked. The leader drew his sword. It was time for Rufus to act and he swung his staff into action, clobbering the hobgoblin hard over his head. To his surprise, the creature only snorted and came towards Rufus with his sword raised. Rufus dodged out of the way as the sword swept past his ear and took another swipe with his staff, hitting the hobgoblin across his neck. Again, the leader merely snorted, shook his head, and advanced on the king. Rufus was not expecting such strength from a hobgoblin and evaded the sword once again; twisting and gripping the end of Caliburn, he swung it with all his might, hitting his attacker square on his back but to no effect at all. The hobgoblin continued to advance.

A change of tactics was needed; Rufus dropped the staff and removed Fireblade from his boot. He dodged the blade again; at least the hobgoblin was slow in movement. Rufus sprang towards the green bulk in front of him and sliced through the creature's stomach. A great roar came from the hobgoblin's mouth as he dropped his sword and held his guts while red gore spurted from the slit made by the knife. Then silence came over the forest as the leader groaned and fell to the ground dead. Rufus glared at the rest of the group, who took one look at the knife and ran back into the forest. Rufus looked down at the dead leader. He'd had no choice but to kill the creature, it was either him or the hobgoblin. With the rest of the group gone, Rufus wiped the blade clean on the jacket of the dead body before returning it to the safety of his boot and retrieving Caliburn. Rufus faced the dilapidated ruin in the clearing, deciding on his next plan of action, when he heard a rustle in the bushes behind him. He turned towards the noise and shouted.

'Come out, I know you are there.' From behind the bush came one of the hobgoblins.

'Don't hurt me,' the hobgoblin pleaded. Rufus gripped Caliburn, ready to strike the creature. 'Please don't hurt me, I want to help you,' the hobgoblin pleaded again. Rufus stared at the hobgoblin, noticing he was one of the group that had taken him prisoner, although, he was much smaller than the others, a young hobgoblin.

'Why do you want to help me?' asked Rufus. 'I have just killed your leader!'

'It was the ogre that made us do the things we did,' claimed the young hobgoblin, 'he terrorised our village and threatened to eat us if we did not do his bidding. I want to help you kill the ogre so that we can get back to our lives and leave you humans in peace, like before the ogre controlled us.' Rufus relaxed his grip on Caliburn but remained suspicious of the creature. 'My name is Percival,' continued the hobgoblin. 'We live in the deepest and darkest part of the forest, away from humans and the like. Then the ogre arrived several months ago, attacking us, bullying my village, making us his slaves, demanding we bring him food and treasures stolen from humans.'

Rufus thought for a moment. Ogres were bad news. The ogre needed to be killed and he was the man to do it. He turned to Percival.

'I need your help to lure the ogre out into the open. Go to the manor and tell him you have a prisoner for him.'

The small hobgoblin saluted Rufus before walking towards the manor.

'Lorac the Ogre,' he called. 'I have a human prisoner for you.' After a short time, the grotesque creature emerged from the wreck of the building. Standing at eight feet tall with a filthy, grey tunic wrapped around his green, scabby skin, the ogre advanced towards Percival.

'Where are your fellows?' bellowed Lorac, 'and where is the human creature?'

Meanwhile, Rufus, out of sight, had tethered Fireblade to the end of Caliburn, preparing himself for one hell of a fight. Ogres were strong and great fighters, never giving up until they were victorious or dead. Rufus took a few deep breaths before emerging from the trees to face Lorac.

'What is this?' demanded the ogre. 'What is going on?' Percival decided it was time to get out of the way and ran to hide in a bush. Rufus stared at the ogre.

'Your time is up,' he called out to the giant. 'Leave this forest now or prepare to die,' the King continued. Lorac looked at the human creature before him, not sure of the seriousness of the situation. Then he laughed.

'Ha, what can a guttersnipe like you do?' With that, he reached over to a nearby tree and wrenched it from the ground. Lorac was now armed with a formidable weapon.

'Shit,' thought Rufus. He was not expecting that.

The ogre swept the tree around, taking a swipe at Rufus. The King managed to leap out of the way just in time. He was going to have trouble getting close enough to the creature to stab him with Fireblade. The ogre took another huge swipe, causing Rufus to duck and jump sideways. Then he leapt forward, preparing to use Caliburn and Fireblade as a spear but just as he pulled his arm back, the tree came flashing back towards him. A branch just clipped his arm, causing him to lose hold of his weapon and throwing him several feet through the air to land on his back. He was winded, his weapon was out of sight, and the ogre was advancing towards him, with the tree above his head, ready to strike. Suddenly from the corner of his eye, Rufus saw Percival materialize from the bushes with Caliburn. The ogre saw the small hobgoblin at the same time. Percival threw the staff towards Rufus just as Lorac swept the tree at the hobgoblin, catching him full on, throwing him into the sky, launching him several yards into the forest. Rufus took the opportunity to grab his weapon and run towards the ogre. Before Lorac realised it, the King was upon him, the blade tethered to the staff had pierced his heart. With a groan the ogre looked at Rufus, before dropping to the ground dead. Rufus retrieved his weapon and went to look for the hobgoblin who had saved his life. He feared the worse for the tiny hero.

Scrambling through deep undergrowth, Rufus headed towards Percival who had landed face down in a bed of nettles.

Rufus reached him, pulling him from the nettles and turning him over, checking for life. He found none. He was aware of movement behind him, which caused him to turn. The other hobgoblins had returned.

'We saw the fight,' called one of the hobgoblins. 'We thank you for ridding us of the ogre,' he continued as they approached, forming a circle around Percival.

'I'm sorry,' whispered Rufus, 'Percival died saving my life.' A tear formed in the corner of his eye as he spoke. 'He is a hero; I will never forget him.'

'It will take more than that to kill a hobgoblin,' stated one of the circle removing a bottle from his bag. He knelt beside the unmoving hero and offered a drink to Percival's mouth. First there was no movement, and then, with a surprise to Rufus, Percival groaned and opened his eyes. The other hobgoblins cheered and patted the youngster on his back as he sat up, none the worse for his escapade. Rufus joined in with the cheering.

Percival was still a little shaken up as he got to his feet, but he had a great big smile on his face because of all the attention he was getting. Rufus gave him a hug, ignoring the rancid stink of the young hobgoblin, and thanked him for saving his life and for being so brave.

'It will soon be dark,' grunted one of the hobgoblins, 'with the death of the ogre we can return to Ringsteade without fear.' He looked at Rufus, 'Join us and celebrate this great day at our camp. Tomorrow we can start getting back to normal: return to our home in the forest and call back our women, who we had sent away. We can enjoy our lives once again.' Rufus looked up at the descending sun in the sky. It would soon be night.

'I would love to join you to celebrate this day,' he replied. The group of unlikely friends marched south through the forest, towards the coast and the camp of the hobgoblins. One of the hobgoblins began singing as they walked:

'Hail the Hero hobgoblin, Percival is his name. He helped the human Rufus bring down the mighty Ogre ...'

THE ISLAND OF THE DEAD

The merriment went on long into the night. Rufus had noticed a large fire across the bay. Percival had told him it was from the Island of the Dead; the home of Mr Belvedore, thought Rufus. As he looked across the bay towards the island, silhouetted against the morning sun, the gentle sea breeze brushing against his face, Rufus was sure he could hear the faint sound of voices. A sort of chanting coming from the small island, or was it just the wind playing tricks with his mind?

Southern voices calling to you, remembered the King; that was how the riddle from the Oracle began:

'Southern voices calling to you, mystic magic seas of blue.' Rufus looked from the cliff edge and decided the sea before him was magic seas of blue. 'Timeless marvels cease to wonder when you know the spell you are under,' Rufus did not know what that meant, at least not yet. Perhaps he would find the answer on the island; it was certainly worth investigating, he thought.

It was as if Percival was reading the King's mind.

'You don't want to go there,' piped up the young hobgoblin. 'Full of druids and crazy people,' he continued, as he bounced towards

Rufus with a cup of nettle tea. Rufus turned away from the sea and faced his new friend,

'You know the place?' enquired Rufus, accepting the clay mug from Percival.

'No, but I know a person who does,' answered Percival, 'a well-to-do lady who has fallen on hard times recently. I'm sure she will be your guide if she is well paid,' he added. Rufus turned back to the island to think. Despite the morning sun, a thin coating of mist had begun to shroud the bottom part of the island. The King had to venture forth and explore the place, but he had no money; Mr Belvedore had put paid to that. Again, it was as if the young hobgoblin had been reading the mind of Rufus.

'You are an honest and good-looking man; I'm sure she would accept an I.O.U. from you,' Percival announced. 'She knows the ways of them strange folk; I heard she has been working with one of the druids that look after the crazies,' he continued.

By now, most of the other hobgoblins had risen from their pits and were either gargling down their mugs of tea or rolling in the wet mud beside the small pond.

'Morning, my friends,' called Rufus. He got snorts and grunts as a reply from the hungover creatures.

Rufus turned back towards Percival and asked how he could find this lady.

'She lives in Wick, just past the town of Waimouthe; a day's walk from here,' stated Percival. 'As your servant, I would like to accompany you and introduce you to Lizzy, the lady in question.'

'You will accompany me as my friend to this Wick place,' announced the King, and together they strode back towards the camp to prepare for their trek along the coast.

The sun was almost at his zenith by the time the two comrades began their trudge west along the cliffs. Clouds had drifted in from the southwest and the mist on the Island of Dead had burnt itself away. It was difficult to look at the island in the glare of the sun. Percival felt proud walking alongside the man and safe in his company, with his staff he called Caliburn with his magic knife tucked away in his boot. Percival had managed to scrounge some strips of coney meat for their journey; the young hobgoblin was going on an adventure. He left his tribe to continue their celebration of the dead ogre and retrieve their womenfolk and children.

The view from a town they stopped at along the way, where Lord Osmond ruled a small community of men and women, was magnificent. The people were suspicious of the odd couple travelling together and refused to let them rest at the local inn, so they sat and ate lunch just outside the village at the bottom of an ancient round barrow. Rufus felt like revealing that he was their king but decided to keep quiet; he did not want word to get out that the king was on an adventure. In a strange kind of way, he enjoyed being a normal man, a traveller on his way to Wick village to meet friends. The new settlement at the mouth of the short river Wai loomed in the distance, with Wick a little further along the coast. 'We will be there long before nightfall,' announced Percival, struggling to pick a strand of coney meat from his yellow, stained teeth.

'I need to spend some time in Waimouthe when we get there,' mumbled Rufus, having trouble chewing the cold, tough, coney meat. 'A friend of mine lives in one of the new houses overlooking the harbour, Lord Godwin. I haven't seen him for years; we used to spend many hours talking about philosophy, the universe and stuff like that.' Percival looked up at Rufus, confused.

'Fillisofy? Onifers?'

'Yes,' Rufus continued, 'Haven't you ever thought of why we are here? Why do we not float off the surface of the planet? What force keeps us firmly planted to the ground, but also allows us to move freely about the surface without much effort?'

'I never thought of anything like that before,' admitted Percival. He imagined himself floating up into the sky and looking down at the land from above. Percival liked the thought and let out a loud, stinking burp in satisfaction to the meal. Rufus was still struggling with his food, while he let his thoughts wander to his old friend Lord Godwin who Rufus knew as the Stag Lord. They had met during weapons training at the New Sarum and hit it off immediately—literally—both were top of the class and shared a liking for a good booze-up in the inns where they would debate the workings of the world. After training, both went their separate ways, exploring their own paths through life.

'He might not be in?' questioned Percival. Rufus pondered for a while before replying to his friend,

'Probably won't be but there is only one way to find out.' He finally managed to swallow the last piece of his meal and washed it down with the last of the water. He must remember to refill the sac at the next river.

The wind had picked up a little by the time the two came to Waimouthe and, amid strange glances, made their way to the harbourside. The small town was bustling with activity: fishermen selling their wares to the locals, early drinkers commuting between the several inns, and the ladies of the night setting up store along the streets, waiting for the many trading ships that spent the night in the harbour. The early evening sun was dropping down towards the western horizon.

'That is Godwin's house, near to the bridge,' Rufus told Percival, pointing to the grandest house on the harbourside. 'The Stag Lord has done well for himself,' thought Rufus. The King had followed the path of his old friend, long after they parted company and was aware that Godwin had spent a lot of time on the Isle of Anglesey, north of Cymru, amongst the druids. If anyone would have some good knowledge of the Priestly Kings, it would be Godwin, and this would help Rufus on his quest over to the Isle of the Dead.

Godwin's wife answered the polished oak door to the unlikely pair on her doorstep. Rufus revealed he was an old friend of her husband without mentioning that he was the ruler of the land.

'Tell him the Holly King would like to see him; he will know who you mean.' Godwin's wife looked at the couple: one tall man, unshaven and unkempt, and a small filthy hobgoblin.

'Why on earth would my husband have anything to do with you two?' she questioned, unsure of the callers. 'Lord Godwin is on his way back from the great circle of stones on the plain, celebrating Beltain with his band, gigging in towns and villages on the way home. I have just had a message that he will be home tonight. You cannot wait for him here though. I am sorry, but I have children to look after. You will have to come back later.'

'My friend and I cannot wait, because we have an appointment in Wick village,' Rufus stated, realising the woman's anxiety. He must look a sight and in the company of a dirty, green, slobbering hobgoblin to boot; who could blame her?

'I will tell him you called when he gets in,' assured Lady Godwin, a little relieved that the pair were not there to hassle her. 'Tell me an address where he could visit you, I am sure the Lord will meet you if he feels it is important.' Rufus turned to Percival for the address of his contact, Lizzy. In a flash, the young hobgoblin revealed that Lizzy resided in the local whorehouse in the centre of Wick. Rufus gulped: he was not expecting that. A frown appeared on Godwin's wife's forehead, but she remained quiet for a time.

'I will tell my husband that the Holly King came looking for him, and that he can find you at the Wick whorehouse tonight.' Rufus rubbed his face in embarrassment and agreed that that was about right. A crying baby could be heard from inside the house, so the adventurers took that as a cue to move on. They walked away in silence; Rufus in an uncomfortable silence, Percival silent because he had nothing to say, just dreaming of floating in the air.

The pair watched the sun sink below the horizon as they reached the village of Wick.

'Where does the sun go, Rufus?' enquired the hobgoblin, as the last rays of Zeus's altar flickered and disappeared behind the large bank of pebbles that joined the Island of the Dead to the mainland, which was half a day's walk along the pebble beach from Abbotsbury.

'The sun journeys to the Underworld, my small friend,' answered Rufus, 'escorting the recently freed souls to their new subterranean reality where they disclose to the Dark Queen what they experienced during their stay in the material world.' Percival did not understand.

'Recently freed souls? I know what a soul is; everything alive has a soul, but dunnit die with the body?'

'No,' Rufus replied. 'Our souls are our real selves; the body is just a shell the soul uses to survive in this world.' Percival tried to get his mind around what Rufus had said. Rufus continued. 'The soul comes into the world to learn about and experience emotions, pain and suffering, and pleasure and love. The soul enters the body at birth and leaves at death to return to its place of learning in the Underworld.'

'The realm of Hades,' interrupted Percival, 'I do know something of what you talk about,' he added.

'Yes,' concluded Rufus, as they reached the doors of the whorehouse. Rufus knocked on the large, oak double doors just as the windows began to show their lights before night closed in. After a short time, the doors opened. A short, stout lady in a pink dress eyed them suspiciously before she spoke, with a trained smile.

'How may I help you?' she asked. Rufus ran his hand through his hair before answering.

'We are looking for Miss Lizzy, the owner of this establishment and friend of my companion here.' He looked down at the hobgoblin beside him. The stout lady in pink was unsure of the nature of the business the pair wanted with her mistress but thought they looked sincere and honest, so she said she would ask if the mistress was free to see them.

'Who shall I say is calling and what is the reason of your visit, may I ask?' Before Rufus could reply, Percival answered.

'We need a guide to take us to the Island of the Dead; we are willing to pay for her services.'

'I see,' said the lady.

'I am Rufus, a tradesman from Vindocladia, and this is Percival. He is from Ringsteade along the coast, and we wish to visit the island for the purpose of trading with the islanders.' The lady saw that they had no goods with them to trade with, but then they could have left their cart around the corner. If they had, it would have been stolen by now if it was unprotected. Anyway, it was none of her business.

'I will see if she is available,' she concluded, and closed the door shut behind her.

Rufus looked up and down the dark street. Small stone buildings stood on both sides of the mud lane. All was quiet, not like the busy Waimouthe around the coast. Rufus turned to Percival.

'How well do you know this lady?'

'I have heard her name mentioned a few times.' Percival replied, 'I have never met her,' the hobgoblin added. Before Rufus could react, the doors opened, and a pretty woman stood on the threshold.

'I am Lizzy Penn,' she announced, 'I hear you need a guide to Portland.'

'Portland? No, we want to go to the Island of the Dead,' responded Rufus.

'Portland is the Island of the Dead,' replied Lizzy, laughing. 'Portland is its real name. Come in,' she offered, 'I have a bit of time, let's talk business.'

Over a cup of Earl Grey, not a taste that the hobgoblin enjoyed much but he went along with the strange ritual anyway, Rufus explained his desire to visit Portland and the riddle that led him there. 'There is a Temple on the east side, overlooking the Ope Cove, but I know nothing of golden cats.' Lizzy explained. 'Anyway, that is only accessible to the druids.

Portland people do not trust strangers; it will be difficult to do business there if you do not know anyone.'

'I know Lord Belvedore,' responded Rufus, 'a dealer in fur'.

'Red Jack', added Percival.

'Everyone knows Jack Belvedore', continued Lizzy, 'not the most popular of men I must say, but it will be enough to get you onto the island.'

Rufus did not realize how tired he felt. He sipped down the last of his tea, turning his attention to Lizzy Penn. The woman was several years younger than Rufus, but a hard life had etched its way into her face. She had a well-to-do air about her and spoke good grammar, showing a good upbringing, but her circumstances had changed. What was she doing running a whorehouse? This was not the time to ask.

'It is where the violent and mad were put,' Lizzy was saying, 'looked after by the druids who live there.'

'What was that?' interrupted Rufus, just catching the words violent, mad, and druids. Lizzy glared at Rufus.

'I said Portland is the place where the crazed and violent are cared for by the druids. Mostly young children whose parents cannot control, and free-thinkers that are kept out of harm's way.'

'Does anyone leave there? I mean, does anyone get cured?' enquired a now-alert Rufus.

'Never,' replied Lizzy, 'That's why they call it the Island of the Dead.'

Percival let out a loud yawn, quickly followed by a short fart.

'I really must be going,' stated Lizzy, rising out of her chair. 'I have work to do. The Smugglers Inn around the corner will put you up for the night. Tell them I sent you; that should ensure a discount. Tomorrow at dawn I will meet you there and escort you to Portland. We can discuss payment then.'

'We haven't any!'

'Thank you for your time, Lizzy,' interrupted Rufus, before his small friend could let it out of the bag that they had no way of paying her, and for that matter no way of paying for a room at the inn.

'You have been most kind and we look forward to seeing you tomorrow.' Rufus put his arm on Percival's shoulder and ushered him out of the house before he could say anything that would create complications. The hobgoblin needed to learn when it was a good time to speak and when to keep quiet. The air had turned cold by the time they left the whorehouse; luckily, the Smugglers Inn was just around the corner. Rufus hoped an understanding landlord ran it.

CROSSING THE CAUSEWAY

The Smugglers Inn was quite busy when Rufus and Percival entered. No one gave them much notice, the Wick people were used to hobgoblins visiting and frequenting the bars. It was one of the few places where man and hobgoblin mixed. Sometimes a troll or two would visit the village, but not tonight. Percival recognised two of the three hobgoblins sat in the corner.

'It's my cousin, Galahad and his buddy Tristan. I don't know the other one,' he remarked to Rufus, who was looking around the room for a place to sit. 'We can join them', Percival insisted and led the way to the table of hobgoblins. 'Hi Galley,' called Percival as they approached, 'This is my friend Rufus. Can we join you?' Galahad let out a loud belch before replying.

'Hi Percy, yes come and join us.' Galahad looked up to the man, 'Hi Rufus, you timed that well, it's Tristan's round; Tristan get my cousin and his friend an ale.' Tristan grunted, picked his nose, and examined the contents before motioning to the barmaid for more ale.

'Thanks Tristan,' said Rufus. Tristan let out another belch before nodding his welcome to the man.

'This is Gawain, my friend,' stated Galahad, putting his hand on the other hobgoblin at the table.

'Hello Gawain,' replied Rufus, as he sat at the table with Percival and the other hobgoblins. The barmaid took Tristan's order and disappeared to the bar.

'I haven't seen you in a while, little cousin,' remarked Galahad, 'What brings you here?'

'We are going to the Island of the Dead tomorrow,' replied Percival. 'We have some business over there.'

'I hope you are taking a guide,' Galahad responded, 'They be a funny lot over there.' Percival proceeded to relate his story so far, of being under the control of the ogre and how Rufus had killed the monster. The barmaid returned with the ales on a tray and waited patiently for Tristan to exchange the five grouts from his purse to her hand. Rufus took a long hard slug of his ale. It went down well.

'Well, well, well, what have we here?' came a voice from behind Rufus. Rufus recognised the voice and turned to see his good friend, Godwin. It was good to see him and the smile that followed showed that. Rufus stood and gave his friend a long hug. 'Jo told me you were in Wick when I reached home. She said you needed to see me and gave your address as the whorehouse. I must admit I was a little surprised, but the maid there told me I could find you here.'

'In the whorehouse, were you Percy?' teased Galahad. 'Yes ... but ... no ... I ... we ... we didn't do anything,' stuttered Percival, going greener with embarrassment.

'You don't have to explain to me young Perce; I understand.'

'No, we were just meeting someone: Lizzy Penn the owner,' replied a flustered Percival. Galahad began to laugh, which set off Tristan and Gawain into snorts of laughter. It brought a smile to the face of Rufus, watching the hobgoblins tease each other.

'We can speak in private, in a back room,' whispered Godwin. 'I have not got long; I have not seen the wife in weeks, so I had better not keep her waiting too long for my company.' Rufus grabbed his keg of ale, which told the hobgoblins that he and his friend needed to speak in private before following Godwin out through the back into a small room. The two old friends sat opposite each other, both taking a large gulp of ale before giving a quick account of where they were along their respective paths, before destiny had brought them together once again.

'I hear you are going to Portland?' asked Godwin. 'Be aware of their ways and respect their customs, and you should be fine. It is probably best to keep your identity secret; the druids do not regard Kings very highly. Kings have tried to rule them for an eternity without success.' Godwin got comfortable in his chair before continuing,

'Rufus the trader needs merchandise; I can arrange a supply of quartz crystals for your use by the morning. The islanders like things like that. As for Jack Belvedore, he is a villain that cannot be trusted. It is better to visit the Druid Bernard. Call him Red Fox and he will understand you are reliable. As for the hobgoblin, are you sure you want to take him? Hobgoblins are seen as a bad omen over there!'

'The hobgoblin, Percival, is a brave and honest creature,' answered Rufus, 'And he saved my life.'

'Ok, if you are sure,' shrugged Godwin. 'What about Fireblade?' he continued, 'Your dagger. Have you got her with you?'

'I always carry her with me.' replied Rufus. Godwin ordered another two ales before continuing.

'All weapons are barred from the island, which is guarded by the sea god Lir. Every caller must face Frag'arach, the Answerer, Lir's sword.'

'I cannot be without Fireblade,' yelled Rufus.

'No problem,' Godwin reassured. 'Because Fireblade was created in the Otherworld she can be hidden from the physical world in the realm of spirit. A mantra will open a pocket in the fabric of space and time into which magical items can be stored away until they are needed again'. Godwin smiled before continuing, 'My path has taken me to some interesting places. I learnt that trick in Nepal, the navel of the world.'

'I have heard of it,' Rufus said, as he lifted the fresh keg of ale to his lips. 'A place I will visit one day,' he assured himself. Godwin continued.

'If it has to be, a physical thing from this world can be hidden. However, to keep the balance of the world intact a certain amount of energy is released from the Otherworld. That power can be either positive or negative energy, or somewhere in between, and will interact with our world until the earth object is recovered. Then it returns to its own realm, leaving its effect to play out on earth. Only use that as a last resort. The longer the energy from the Otherworld is in our world, the more chaos it can create. Sometimes, the thing is never recovered for whatever reason, and our world descends a little more into an eternal state of chaos.'

By the time the ale was drunk, Rufus had mastered the art of hiding Fireblade in the Otherworld.

'I have had a word with the landlord, and your rooms for the night have been paid for. As I said, a bag of quartz crystals will be here for you at sunrise. I had better get home now. Come in and see me when you return to the mainland.' Godwin pulled a purse from his pocket and handed Rufus several silver coins, 'You will need these my friend.' Godwin concluded, hugging his good friend Rufus.

'Thank you, James,' replied Rufus, hugging his friend back, and giving him the secret handshake before leaving the backroom.

Rufus collected Percival from the bar, thanked and bid farewell to Galahad, Tristan, and Gawain before heading up to their rooms, and hopefully to good comfortable mattresses.

Rufus slept well on the warm comfortable bed, but Percival found his too soft and too warm, and he was not used to sleeping on his own. He found the whole experience an uncomfortable one. The landlord put on a good breakfast for the pair to feast on before their trek to Portland, and a bag of quartz crystals was waiting for Rufus. It had been delivered to the inn while they ate. When they had finished, Rufus stored Fireblade in the Otherworld like he was shown, before waiting outside for Lizzy. She was late. A blanket of grey cloud that threatened rain covered the morning sky and with it came a cool breeze. Rufus pulled his cloak tight around his shoulders. A short while later, Lizzy came around the corner carrying a large backpack. 'My wares,' she told Rufus, as she approached. 'I have business with

Fedel'ma, the prophetess: animal bones for her divinations.'

'I have quartz crystals to sell,' Rufus told Lizzy. Percival scratched his tired head, wondering if he should have had something to trade.

'What about me?' he asked. 'I have nothing.'

'You can carry our bags.' Lizzy said, 'Your reason for visiting Portland is as our servant.' She passed her bag of bones to him. 'Give him your bag, Rufus,' Lizzy continued. Rufus felt guilty, using his friend as a servant but Percival accepted his position with enthusiasm. 'No weapons of any kind are allowed on the island,' stressed Lizzy, as she arranged the bags over the hobgoblin's shoulders.

'We have no weapons.' replied Rufus, pulling his hood over his head to combat the cool breeze that made its way up the street.

'What about your staff?' Lizzy queried, 'That is a weapon.'

'I cannot be without my staff.' replied Rufus. 'I will say I need it as a crutch for my bad leg.'

'You will have to do better than that,' countered Lizzy, 'the ferryman is not stupid.' Lizzy went into the inn and returned a short while later with a large wooden cudgel. Before Rufus could ask what, it was for, Lizzy swung it down hard onto Rufus's right leg, causing him to let out a yelp.

'What did you do that for?' he screamed at the woman.

'So, you can genuinely take your staff onto the island as a crutch.' Lizzy replied. 'As I said, the ferryman is not stupid.' While Rufus rubbed his painful leg, Lizzy returned the cudgel to the inn.

Soon the trio were making their way down the street, towards the small ferry that would take them across to the Island of the Dead. The ferryman was waiting for them.

'A penny from each of you,' growled the boatman. Both Lizzy and Percival looked to Rufus. Rufus took three pennies from his purse and handed them to the ferryman. The ferryman placed the coins into his coat pocket and looked hard at the staff.

'This is my crutch,' explained Rufus and pulled up his trouser leg to show the ferryman his bruise.

'It is not for me to judge,' replied the ferryman, 'I leave that to Lir, the protector god of the island.' With that, the ferryman invited the group aboard his boat and set off to the other side. It was a short journey, but the current was very strong, too strong for anyone to wade or swim across. Rufus wondered how the ferryman could keep the boat from being pulled from its path. Soon they were on the other side and standing on the Portland shingle, looking at the island in the distance at the far end of a long causeway.

'The people take their guidance from the druids,' explained Lizzy. 'It was the great Archdruid Verne who raised the island from the sea many hundreds of years ago. A dolmen dedicated to the Archdruid stands at the top of the island.' Lizzy told Rufus and Percival as they began to make their way along the rough path that led to the great lump of limestone before them. As they walked, the sky grew darker and drops of rain began to fall. Seagulls flew above them, crying out a warning to the island people that they had visitors. They were soaked to the skin by the time they reached the base of the rock known as the Island of the Dead. Small dwellings scattered the base of the hill all the way down to the pebble beach. Above the stone huts, a little way up the hill, Rufus spotted a tavern, and the trio made their way towards it.

'We need to get out of this foul weather and dry off,' exclaimed Rufus, aware they were being stared at by the locals that had come out of their huts to look at the new arrivals. They were not welcoming looks. They had seen Lizzy on several occasions and had accepted her presence, but the man and hobgoblin looked like trouble to them. Rufus tried to make eye contact with the locals, to try and show he was not a danger to them, but the islanders lowered their heads and returned to their homes out of the rain. They knew that if they were trouble, the druids would deal with them.

Rufus's leg hurt; Lizzy had made too good a job of that. He really did need his staff to support himself. Drops of rain dripped from his nose.

'I will let you dry off at the Star Inn,' Lizzy said, 'while I visit the Prophetess Fedel'ma. Her fairy mound is up on the west cliffs at the top of the hill. I will not be long, about an hour or so, then I shall return and take you to see the Druid Bernard. Keep yourselves out of trouble.' She took her bag of bones from Percival and continued past the Star, towards the cliffs. Rufus and Percival entered the tavern; a crowd of locals stared in silence at them when they entered the bar. Rufus ignored them and made his way to the bar.

'Two ales please, barman,' Rufus asked, giving his cloak a shake in an attempt to remove the wetness.

'We do not serve hobgoblins here,' growled the barman, 'or their companions,' he added. Rufus looked hard at the barman. He was not used to this kind of abuse. He asked again but more forcefully this time.

'I would like two ales, barman, and I am not leaving until I receive them.' The sound of chairs moving behind him made him turn around. Six burly Portlanders had stood up, one or two armed with cudgels.

'Strangers do not demand anything on this island,' one of them shouted. 'Prepare for a good hiding, mainlander.' Rufus raised his hands to subdue the situation.

'Please, we do not want any trouble; we will leave.'

'Too late for that,' replied the biggest man in the group, and moved towards the two visitors. Rufus prepared himself with Caliburn at the ready as the men lunged forward. The fight did not last long. The Portland men lay dazed and bleeding on the floor, tables were upturned, and crockery broken. The rest of the drinkers had fled the tavern when the fight started; they ran to inform the druids. The mainlander and the green monster would be punished. It was time to leave. Outside the tavern, a crowd had gathered to see the commotion caused by the two strangers. Rufus pushed his way through the people, with Percival close behind, and they made their way towards the northern slopes that faced the mainland. They had only been on the island for a short time and were already fugitives. Rufus had noticed from the causeway that the northern slope was covered in greenery, with caves further up the cliff. He needed to hide and reassess his plans. At least the rain had eased as he and Percival left the small village at the mouth of the causeway behind them. At least for now, nobody was following.

By the time Rufus and Percival had found somewhere to lie low in a ruined stone building, hidden from view by gorse bushes and small hawthorns. The sun was high in the sky and threatening to emerge from the grey clouds. Rufus and Percival gathered twigs and soon a warm fire was burning inside their shelter.

'I shouldn't have come,' groaned Percival, 'It is all my fault.' Rufus put a reassuring hand on his friend's shoulder.

'Do not blame yourself, my friend.' Rufus replied. 'You wanted an adventure, and no adventure is without its setbacks.' Percival smiled. Steam rose from their clothing as they huddled around the fire.

'What are we going to do now?' asked Percival. Rufus thought for a while; he did not really have a plan. The reason he was here was to solve the riddle from the Oracle and confront Red Jack, who had robbed him. First, he would ask the Goddess for guidance, and then hunt a coney or two for lunch.

While Rufus was in communication with his goddess, Percival was sent out to capture some conies, hunting being a special talent of all hobgoblins. A weak sun had penetrated the grey cloud by the time Percival returned with two conies. Rufus stoked up the fire, while Percival skinned and prepared the conies for cooking.

HARD LABOUR

With a full stomach Rufus could think much clearer. Lizzy would have returned to the Star by now and learnt of the disturbance they had caused. It was best to keep her out of things; Rufus did not want to get her involved and in trouble with the druids. The best thing to do was to try and contact the Druid Bernard somehow.

'What are druids?' asked Percival suddenly.

'Druids are priests that maintain the running of the community and see to the spiritual needs of the people.' Rufus replied. 'They love and respect nature, and acknowledge the cycles of life, death, and rebirth. They plan their lives according to the path of the sun's movement around the earth and chart the phases of the moon for the best times to do their magic work. Events in the heavens reflect what is happening on the earth.' Percival pondered on what Rufus had said. He did not fully understand it but liked to hear new things about the strange world he lived in. Before Rufus could continue, a shout came from beyond the ruined walls of their shelter. Three druids stood outside, white robes flowing in the breeze, each armed with a crystal-adorned staff pointing towards the fugitives. 'That is a druid,' whispered Rufus, as he stood peering over the dilapidated wall. They did not look at all friendly.

'Come with us or face the consequences,' one of them shouted. Rufus knew the power the druids had over the elements and decided to agree to their request. He did not stop them from taking Caliburn away from him. He was aware of the power of the druids and knew resisting them was futile.

Rufus and Percival were marched up to the top of the hill, into a fortress protected by two banks and ditches surrounded by a wooden palisade. Twenty or so huts were spread out inside the hill fort. At the centre of the fortification stood a large dolmen. Fires were being lit as the sun descended towards the horizon. Dogs barked at the new arrivals and people stared as the druids ushered the two prisoners towards a large hut near to the dolmen.

'Stay here,' one of the druids commanded, as he entered the large wooden hut that had a thatched roof. The other two druids stood motionless each side of the prisoners.

'I'm scared,' whispered Percival.

'Do not be frightened my small friend,' replied Rufus, 'druids are known for their justice and wisdom.' He continued, 'I will explain everything to them; we will be fine.'

'Quiet,' ordered the druid standing next to Rufus, his white gown ruffling in the strong wind that coursed its way across the top of the hill.

From the top of the hill Rufus could see the entire island, from its southern tip towards the Beale to the northern hill behind him that swept steeply down to the protective cove, and the great bank of pebbles that swept north westwards as far as the eye could see.

'Face the front,' ordered the druid. Rufus returned his gaze to the hut. Soon, the druid who had entered the hut earlier returned and motioned for Rufus to enter.

'Not you, hobgoblin,' the druid ordered, as Percival began to follow his friend. Inside the hut Rufus found it difficult to see anything in the darkness. His eyes soon grew accustomed to the dimness, and he became aware of the white-robed druid examining something on a table in front of him. On each side of the druid was a priestess, both dressed in light blue, flax cotton dresses. Their long, black hair and heavily made-up eyes made them look like the whores who sold their bodies back in Vindocladia. The druid finished examining the bones that were laid on the table and looked up at Rufus.

'I am Rufus,' started the captive, before the druid hushed him with a wave of his hand. The pair stared at each other for what seemed like an eternity before the druid spoke. His voice was almost a whisper, making it difficult for Rufus to hear him.

'I am the Druid Balise,' he spoke slowly, 'I am the person who decides the fate of troublemakers on this island.' Rufus opened his mouth to speak but once again was silenced by the wave of the druid's hand. Another spate of silence followed. 'I know who you are,' the druid finally continued. 'You are King Rufus of Vindocladia. What I do not know is why you are here. The bones are giving mixed messages: nothing unscrupulous but nevertheless a confusing connotation, which is not a good thing. You seek treasure? You seek revenge? You seek something that does not exist in this realm?' Rufus remained silent. Druid Balise brushed the bones from the table into a small leather pouch and handed it to one of the priestesses. She tucked the bag into her belt, muttering a mantra as she did so. She bowed to the druid and left the hut. Balise turned to the second priestess, and she handed him a leather pouch, which she removed from her belt. Balise uttered a mantra as he shook the bag and tipped its contents onto the table. The bones dropped haphazardly in front of him. When they settled, the druid stared at them intently for a time before turning to the priestess. To Rufus it seemed that the pair were communicating telepathically: a nod here, a movement of the hand there, another nod. Finally, the priestess turned her head to the floor while the druid looked Rufus in the eye. 'The reason you have been brought here to me is for the disruption you caused in the Star Inn. On your arrest, the more serious crime of killing and eating two conies was discovered. Rufus thought of saying something but knew it was not a good idea to answer until he was asked to do so. Since when was it a crime to hunt and eat wild animals? he thought. It was his right; it was the right of all men to hunt the land for food.

'The Gods and Goddesses have decreed that your punishment for killing an animal sacred to this isle is seven days hard labour in the quarries,' Balise stated, 'and an extra day for causing a disruption in the Star Inn.' He continued, 'Guards, take him away.'

'Wait a minute,' protested Rufus, as two of the druids who had brought him there entered the hut and grabbed him by the shoulders. Rufus shook them free, determined to get his point across. Balise raised his hand and Rufus was taken over by a strange paralysis. He was unable to move; his body was frozen, and his voice refused to work.

The two druids marched Rufus down the slope, southwards towards a large enclosure near to the east cliffs. Rufus was still unable to speak but he had regained the use of his legs, not that he had any control of them. They seemed to be working by themselves.

'Welcome to Portland prison,' one of the druids spoke, as a large wooden door opened to let them through. Once inside, the spell that had overcome him disappeared, allowing Rufus to curse under his breath and regain control of his faculties. A giant of a man greeted them and told Rufus to follow him. For a second Rufus thought of refusing but decided against it.

'Where is my friend, the hobgoblin?' Rufus demanded.

'The hobgoblin has been sent to work in the Infirmary at the Beale,' replied the giant man. 'He will be helping to care for the unfortunates that have been sent here.'

'The mad you mean?' questioned Rufus. The prison warden stopped and turned towards Rufus.

'The people brought to the island are not mad, just different,' replied the warden. 'They are the people that society will not or cannot control. Here, we work with them to try and understand their difference and enable them to use it in a controlled manner. These people are in communication with the gods; their rantings are messages from the heavens. We help them understand the voices in their heads, and in turn they help us understand the wishes of the gods.' The warden turned and headed towards a large hut. Rufus followed.

Inside, a candlelit the room, full of stone and bone tools used for quarrying. The giant man was the warden; he told Rufus to change into a pair of grey trousers and jacket emblazoned with arrows, which showed he was a prisoner.

'It is too late in the day for you to start work,' stated the warden. 'It will soon be time to eat. Once you are changed, come and see me in my hut at the centre of the yard.' The warden left, leaving Rufus alone. He looked around the musty room. His first thought was to escape and get away from this crazy place, but he decided against it. He checked to see if Fireblade was still accessible; it was, but he left it where it was for the moment. For now, he would play along with his captors; there was not much else he could do right now. The grey uniform made his skin itch. It was not the first time Rufus had been imprisoned: two years earlier he had been captured by the Picts when he ventured into the Northern lands. He had spent a cycle of the moon tied to a post, until his father had paid the ransom for his release. There was no chance of help now; his people did not know where he was. He hoped that Lizzy would inform his friend Godwin, or even have a word with the Druid Bernard. But for now, all he could do was kill time and see what awaited him. When he was ready, he exited the hut. The sun was low in the western sky and the aroma of cooking reached his nose. Other prisoners were coming in through the gate and making their way to a long hut along the eastern wall. Rufus walked to the end hut where the giant man had asked him to go and from the entrance called out to the warden.

'Enter,' came the reply. Rufus pulled back the heavy sack drape that covered the entrance and went in. Animal skulls and bones hung from the wall and rafters, furs were spread about the room and bowls of various types of plant material lay on the floor. The smell made Rufus wince and his eyes water. 'You may be a King in the outside world, but here you are a prisoner with no purpose other than to quarry stone. You have no name, only a number: that of 666.' The warden stared at Rufus to ensure he understood his fate for the next eight days. 'Do you understand?'

'Yes,' answered Rufus.

'Yes Sir,' commanded the warden.

'Yes Sir,' replied Rufus. He was getting tired now; it had been a long day.

'I will take you to the rectory to eat, then you will retire to the hut that you will share with six other prisoners to get some sleep. In the morning, you will be taken to the cliffs where you will work in the quarry. Do you understand?' 'Yes Sir.'

The warden led Rufus across the yard, where he joined the other prisoners lining up for their food. The queue moved in silence towards a group of men dishing out, what looked to Rufus, a stew of some kind that surprisingly smelt good. Once he had sat with the other thirty or so prisoners, a druid stood at the end of the tables and began to address the men. 'Let us dedicate our meal to the

Goddess,' he commenced. 'Let us begin by giving peace to the quarters, for without peace there is no pleasure in what we do.' The druid turned to the North and raised his hands, 'Peace to the East.' The prisoners responded by chanting 'Peace to the East.' Peace to the South, West and North followed, ending with everyone calling for peace throughout the whole world.

'Now repeat with me the Druids' Prayer,' the druid continued.

'Grant, O Goddess thy protection,
And in protection, Strength,
And in strength, Understanding,
And in understanding, Knowledge,
And in knowledge, the Knowledge of Justice,
And in the knowledge of Justice, the Love of it,
And in the love of it, the Love of all Existences,
And in the love of all existences, the Love of Goddess and all Goodness'.
'Blessed be.'

As soon as the prayer had finished, all the prisoners at once began to eat their food from the wooden bowls. Rufus joined in and was pleased the food tasted as good as it smelt. Bread was handed out by priestesses, which was used to wipe the bowls clean. Afterwards Rufus tried to make conservation with those around him, only to be told to keep quiet or else suffer another day added to his sentence. The priestesses collected the empty bowls and gave out clay mugs of mead to wash it all down.

By the time they had finished, darkness had descended over Portland and the prisoners began to leave the rectory. A skinny, bearded man in prison uniform approached Rufus. '666, you are with me. I am 425, chief of the Crow gang. Follow me.' Without a word, Rufus followed the man back to one of the huts. Inside, five other men had already settled under their furs preparing to sleep. 'Best grab yourself a fur and get straight to sleep,' 425 recommended. 'Quarry work is hard work and tomorrow we will be up at sunrise and going straight to the cliffs to break the stone.' Rufus was too tired to talk. It would probably be frowned upon anyway, so he found a fur and crept into it and before he knew it, was in the land of nod.

A horn echoed around the prison as the sun began his ascent into the heavens. Rufus stirred, rubbed his eyes and it took a while before he remembered where he was. The hut stank, so it was no effort for Rufus to get up. The early morning air was cold; the thin prison uniforms were no good against the chilly air. The men from the Crow gang gathered their wits in silence and followed 425 out into the yard, to line up alongside the other gangs. A morning prayer was chanted, before a druid led the prisoners out of the yard towards the eastern cliffs. Rufus was taken aback at the beauty he witnessed as the sun reflected his light across the sea towards him. The yellow and orange sky brought calm to the mind of Rufus despite the anguish of what lay before him. His gang was led by 425 to the bottom of the cliff, to stand amongst a mass of stones. 425 explained that the stone was the remains of the chippings hacked off by the Otter gang, who prepared and smoothed the stone before it was transported either for building or carving. It was the job of the Crow gang to smash the stone into chippings used for pathways around the island. Each man was given a hammer of granite to pulverise the Portland stone into gravel. Priestesses wandered among the men, offering water to anyone that needed it. Soon sweat poured from Rufus as the sun warmed the morning air and the hammering began to take its toll. It was hard graft. A priestess came to offer Rufus a drink. She whispered as Rufus sipped from the clay jug,

'Lizzy is trying to gain your freedom. She is seeking a hearing from the Druidess Birog, who has clout with the chief druid.'

'Has she any chance?' asked Rufus.

'Lizzy is well-respected on the island,' the priestess replied, 'She is doing good work with caring for the unfortunates at the Beale. The druids have great respect for her but take nothing for granted. If anything is to happen, it will take a few days.' A druid called out to the priestess to move on. Rufus thanked her and carried on smashing the hard Portland stone. His arms were beginning to ache already.

At noon, a horn blasted to let it be known it was time for a short break, and priestesses brought round bread rolls with the water for the men. It was a welcome rest for Rufus. He was not sure he could keep this up for the rest of the day, let alone for eight days. Suddenly, a scream took his attention away from his thoughts. Close by, one of the prisoners had a druid pinned against a large stone, with a flint blade at his throat. The prisoner was demanding his freedom or else the druid would get it. Without a thought for his own safety, Rufus leapt towards the prisoner, pulling the blade away from the druid, and wrestling the prisoner to the floor. The prisoner waved the blade frantically, slashing Rufus across his chest. It was enough time for the druid to gain his composure and retrieving his staff, shot a bolt of energy into the frenzied knife-wielding prisoner, killing him instantly. Rufus groaned in agony as the blood surged from his chest. A priestess was soon at hand to tend to his wound.

Two of the Crow gang helped Rufus up the cliff to the hospital inside the prison, accompanied by the priestess. The cut was deep, but the priestess had managed to stem the flow of blood and had administered a concoction of herbs to take away the pain. Rufus fell into a deep sleep.

SWAN FEATHER

It was dark when Rufus came round. He felt the comfort of a soft mattress beneath him and a loose, flax blanket covering him. He felt drowsy as he tried to identify his surroundings. The twinge in his chest reminded him of his recent exploits. He remembered being helped up the cliff and taken into the prison. He could not remember anything after that.

Rufus sat up as his eyes adjusted to what little light penetrated the room. The light was from a fire in a room on the other side of the doorway. A soft white material protected his wound; at least Rufus felt he was being well looked after. He found his clothes, well, his prison trousers anyway and boots. His top was most likely ruined by the blade cut and blood. Rufus exited the room into the room with the glow. At the centre of the room, a fire was burning in a cauldron, lighting the space enough for Rufus to see that there were other rooms off this one. A breeze blew open a light sheet, which covered the main door for a few moments. It was dark outside. The room he stood in was like a community hall, with groups of tables and chairs dotted around the space. Rufus edged his way to the door, expecting to be challenged by someone at any moment, but nobody came. Rufus slipped past the door curtain and into the cool air. The full moon shone bright in the eastern sky. Rufus found the constellation of Cygnus, the destination of the soul in the afterlife. At the head of the swan constellation was the star Deneb that showed Rufus where North was. In the other direction, the stars of Drago watched.

    From behind the building Rufus could hear soft voices amongst the gentle breeze that ruffled the newly blossomed beech leaves. Silently, he crept around the building towards the voices. As he crept closer, he could tell the voices were chanting, very softly but a definite rhythm could be made out. Pulling back the leaves of a bush, Rufus was shocked at what he saw in the moonlight. Twenty yards away was a stone circle, consisting of around a dozen waist-high monoliths equally spaced around a diameter of about five steps. Pacing around the stones were a group of women, naked beneath their flowing cloaks apart from a leather pouch nestling between their breasts. Some carried candles, others carried bowls and baskets of stuff. 'Witches,' thought Rufus. He watched as the High Priestess led them into the circle from the east and walked sunwise inside the stones, until each witch had settled at their given direction. Four witches stood at each of the direction stones and two in between each of them. One by one, starting with the High Priestess at her station in the north, in charge of the altar, each witch in turn placed what they had brought with them onto it and returned to their position.

The breeze that welcomed Rufus when he left the building had dropped, making everything still, everything quiet. Rufus hoped the witches would not hear his heart pounding in his chest, bringing out the pain from his wound. He had a new scar to show to his friends.

Rufus watched the High Priestess touch the ground with her palms. He saw the white glow of her energy flow out of her into the ground and return moments later, fused with the golden energy of the Earth. With the new energy inside her, she stood upright and unbuckled her cloak, letting it fall against the stone she represented, exposing her naked flesh that for Rufus reflected the beauty of nature itself. The other witches also allowed their cloaks to drop to the ground.

Rufus watched in awe as the High Priestess gathered a besom from beside her altar and started to sweep away the dark, negative energies that lurked at the edges of the circle. While she swept, she called to the spirit world.

'As I sweep, may the besom chase away all evil spirits from this circle so that it may be fit for my work.'

The besom was returned to the altar, the candles and incense bowls lit, and brought to life with a little magic from the High Priestess;

something she learnt at the Academy of Avebury. With her energy rising, the High Priestess called to the spirit world.

'The circle is about to be cast, and I stand freely within it to greet the Goddess Nemonta and the God Nodens.'

The High Priestess took a candle from the altar, raised it to the heavens, and faced towards Deneb, which hovered over Waimouthe on the mainland. She was facing Rufus, but her attention was towards the heavens. Rufus could not help looking at her naked body, glowing in the silver moonlight that shone, lighting the stone circle. Her dark hair, adorned with dandelions and daisies, swept behind her small but strong shoulders. She had a lean but muscular body; her breasts looked the to the Earth elementals to come and strengthen the circle.'

The High Priestess proceeded to the East stone, raised the candle high and looked out across the dark sea, calling to the spirits that dwelt there.

'I call to the East upon the light to the Air elementals to come and invigorate the circle.'

The priestess then strides to the South stone,

looking down the gentle slope towards the Beale on the southern tip of the island. She raises the candle high as she calls,

'I call to the South upon the light to the Fire elementals to come and warm the circle'.

The priestess reached the final direction stone, facing West over the fields of produce that would sustain the island people during the winter months. The candle was raised up as the priestess called once again,

'I call to the West upon the light to the Water elementals to come and cleanse the circle.'

With all the stations called, the priestess returned to her altar for her athame, her sacred twin-bladed dagger, used like a wand for transforming the energy that was being created. She took several deep breaths, slowly inhaling and exhaling, each breath stilling her mind further. Then she turned inwards, towards the centre of the circle.

Rufus watched as the Earth's golden energy rise up through the bare feet of the priestess and up her legs to her root chakra at the base of her spine, which shone red on contact. Instinct was awakened. The energy continued to rise, opening the sacral chakra causing it to emit an orange glow. Passion awoke. The yellow shine of the solar plexus in the higher stomach was next to open. Self-esteem was awake. The Earth energy continued to rise, turning the heart into a green, pulsating light. Compassion was awake. The throat chakra turned a radiant blue, awakening Expression, before resting awhile in the purple glare of the third eye chakra and having a moment with the awakening Perception. The energy reached the crown chakra, the Temple of Love. A violet luminance wakes, triggering the opening of the gate between the priestess and the universe.

The priestess raised the athame towards the heavens, drawing energy from the crown chakra and sending it towards Heaven. She called to the Gods and Goddesses,

'I draw this circle in the honour and presence of Nemonta and Nodens so they will aid and bless my magic.'

Turning to her left as she began her circuit of the circle, a blue light flowing from the tip of the athame traced the steps of the priestess. A blue ring of protection hovered in the air, revealing the boundary to the magical area. As the priestess walked, she called to the heavens,

'This is the boundary of the circle. It is around me; it is above me and below me creating a ball of divine energy that Nemonta and Nodens will work through me: their child, Swan Feather. This circle is charged by the powers of the Ancient Ones. Only love can enter and only love will leave.'

Returning to the altar, the priestess blessed the salt with the athame. A white pulse of energy formed in the heart of Swan Feather and travelled to her arms, through the athame into the bowl of salt.

'Salt is life and purifies. I bless the salt so that it can be used in this sacred circle by the Powers of the Goddess and the God.'

Three portions of salt are transferred with the athame into a bowl of spring water, from near to the Temple of Venus overlooking the cove. The white energy turned the water a glowing white when it was stirred by the blade three times.

'Let the blessed salt purify this water so that it can be used in this sacred circle. Through the powers of the Goddess and God this water is blessed.'

Swan Feather proceeded to scatter the charged water around the circle with her fingers. Flashes of light sprang from her hands, showering the ground inside the circle with a ghostly glimmer.

'I consecrate this circle through Nemonta and Nodens. It is a circle of Power that is purified and sealed. So, Mote it Be.'

With the bowl of incense, Swan Feather honoured and made welcome her friends and helpers, both visible and invisible, patiently waiting in the circle. Then she used her fingertip to draw a pentagram on her forehead with anointing oil.

'I, Swan Feather am consecrated in the names of Nemonta and Nodens in this, their circle.'

The energy in the circle intensified; a low throb vibrated inside the circle, sending waves of energy up through the bare soles of the coven and into their bodies to their crown chakras. A silver mist filled the circle and particles of colour spun this way and that.

A cold breeze brushed across Rufus's bare back, causing him to shiver. He rubbed his eyes in disbelief at what he was witnessing. Despite feeling the cold, a warm sweat swept down his face. His heart was racing, and he was beginning to breathe heavily. He had to move from his kneeling position to sit down and try to control his breathing, or else he would pass out. Rufus cursed his carelessness when he snapped a twig as he resumed his kneeling position. Neither the witches nor the sentinels had taken any notice of the noise—it seemed he had gotten away with it.

It took several moments before he wrestled control of his breathing and slowed down his heart. The sweat on his face felt cold in the south-easterly wind, which helped settle Rufus. He returned his attention to the witch ritual.

Swan Feather had anointed herself with a pentagram on her forehead and had cut a doorway in the fabric of time and space with the athame. She was questioning each witch in turn before allowing them through to join her in the spiritual realm.

'What do you want?' she asked,
'To enter the circle,' was the reply.

'What is the password?' Swan Feather requested,

'In perfect love and perfect trust,' came the confident reply. Swan Feather anoints each witch with the sign of Venus on her forehead and ushers her in through the gateway, closing the gate behind her.

'Enter with a free mind and a free will. I bid you welcome.'

Each witch circles the stones before returning to her original position, while the High Priestess opens the gate to the next witch in line. When all twelve witches had passed through the gateway and settled in their stations, Swan Feather continued. She picked up her hazel wand, she had made it herself, and it had been blessed by the Archdruidess Mor'iath at the New Sarum last solstce. She was looking forward to feeling its power. She turned towards the North, towards the constellation of Cygnus, hovering over the hills on the mainland. She is aware of the bright glow of the Moon to her right, looking down on them. It would be her turn to enter the ritual soon, but first she needed to bring the elementals to the party. She led the coven in raising their arms in welcome to the North. Swan Feather requested an audience,

'I call upon the element of Earth to be present at this ritual and guard this circle. With my body and strength, you and I are one.'

The energy at the North stone began to grow brighter and solidify into a powerful brown bear. He was the guardian of the North Quarter and would ensure that no evil energy could come in from the North.

The coven turned to the East, to raise the Eastern elementals.

'I call upon the element of Air to be present at this ritual and guard this circle. As I breath and think, you and I are one.'

The energy at the East stone transformed into a hawk that soared into the air and circled down to perch on the East stone to protect the East Quarter. The Southern elementals were then hailed.

'I call upon the element of Fire to be present at this ritual and guard this circle. With my energy and drive, and my love of life, you and I are one.'

A stag, majestic in form, materialised from the energy in the circle. Standing fast and alert, he was ready for his duties of protecting the South Quarter.

The last of the directions were called towards the West.

'I call upon the element of Water to be present at this ritual and guard this circle. As I have emotions and a beating heart, you and I are one.'

An otter appeared from the energy next to the West stone. He looked around at all the faces looking at him and felt honoured that he had been called to be in such company. The otter leapt on to the West stone, assuring that nothing bad could enter from the west on this beautiful night.

The coven rests for a short while, to take in and get accustomed to the new arrivals. It was a warm night for this time of year. The stars glistened and the moon glowed, creating dark moon shadows across the landscape. No shadows penetrated inside the circle.

The High Priestess traced the infinity sign over the altar with her wand before changing it for her athame. Holding it with both hands, the priestess pointed the blade towards the heavens, towards the Otherworld.

'Hail to the Elementals at the four stations. Welcome Nemonta and Nodens to this circle! I stand at the threshold between the two worlds with Love and Power all around me.'

Swan Feather takes a few heavy breaths to concentrate her mind further. A distant rumble from the thunder God, Taranis, echoes far out to the east, following the Moon across the sky. The priestess is aware of the waves crashing gently against the cliffs below. She heard the rustling of the new leaves from the elms and beeches nearby as a breeze drifted by. Then she heard a twig snap somewhere near to her home. Someone, or something, was watching them. She did not sense it to be a threat, more of a brotherly sort of protection. There was much to do tonight; the spying presence could wait. The High Priestess immersed herself back into the magic circle, pouring herself a mug of mead from the clay jug. She drank half and tipped the rest to the ground, as an offering to the earth for her assistance in the magic to be performed. She picked up her wand and, with her arms out to her sides, Swan Feather turned to the Moon, as the Mother Goddess, reflecting her white light across the dark waters towards them and bathing the circle in her light. It was time to include her energy into the mix.

'Welcome the Great Lady who travels the sky with the stars as her attendants lighting up the shadow of night.'

The priestess brings her arms around to address the Moon spirits.

'Beautiful Lady, known by so many names, but known to me as Nemonta with the Lord Nodens as Sol, I give you honour and reverence and invite you to join this circle on this, your special night. Descend my Lady and speak with your child, Swan Feather.'

A silver haze drifts into the circle causing the energy to rotate sunwise, stirring up the mix a little: blending Earth, Spirit, and Consciousness together. Flashes of static electricity jumped from one plane to another, causing sparks to leap across the standing stones from time to time. A yellow light bathed the circle, then a green one, then a blue one. The energy increased its speed until a vortex was created. It materialised from the top as a small puff of black smoke that hovered over the centre of the circle.

Swan Feather told the women that it was time to charge the crystals. If what the Prophetess Fedel'ma had been saying—that a warlock invasion force from Armorica was on the way—the witches' crystals needed to be ready. She had told the coven to bring the most fearsome crystal they had to the circle. The coven removed their crystals from the pouches around their necks and followed the High Priestess in placing them at the centre of the circle, before returning to their stations. The magic is about to begin.

MOON MAGIC

Swan Feather rolled her shoulders in preparation to draw down the energy from the heavens; she took a deep breath before beginning the ritual. She tightened her grip on the wand she held in her right hand and addressing the centre of the circle, she calls to the universe.

'God of Mars and Goddess of Venus, I call down the moon to empower our stones.'

The priestess circles the wand around her head while dancing around the crystals, calling to the planet energies.

'Power of Luna, Power of Venus, and Power of Sol. I call on your powers to use in this circle of magic.'

Swan Feather continues to dance and chant around the crystals, raising her voice and pace as she circles. The energy inside her explodes up through her chakras, up her arm, and through her wand and follows a spiral path up towards the Moon. When the red energy spiral reaches the aura of the moon, she responds by sending her radiance to meet the energy from earth. On contact, the Moon's white light journeys down the red spiral to the wand. A pink glow emanates around the tip of the wand, the energy crackling and buzzing. Swan Feather knows it is time. She grips the wand with both hands and brings it down, pointing it at the crystals.

'In the name of Luna, GIVE POWER TO OUR CRYSTALS.'

A stream of pink energy flows out of the wand and hits the crystals, making them spark and glow in different colours. The priestess continues the transfer of energy for as long as she dares. Too short a time and the crystals are weak, too much and the priestess could pass out, even possibly die if she loses too much energy. She could feel the energy pulsating out of her body and combining with the Mother Goddess. She feels it leaving the wand and entering the crystals. Her skin shivers and her body shakes; the priestess is on the verge of blacking out. Her inner energy is almost depleted, just a few more seconds. Swan Feather grits her teeth for one last effort, before releasing her hold on the Moon's pull. With her hands on her knees, the priestess enjoys some deep breaths and gives herself the chance to wind down.

When she was ready, she turned to the moon, raising her hands above her head. She calls to Earth's satellite.

'You are the mother of all: Maiden, Mother, and Crone. You are at life's beginning and at its end. You dwell inside us, for you are Life and Love, and that makes us Life and Love. Love is the Law, and the Law is Love.'

The magic work was over. The coven reclaim their crystals from the centre of the circle. They are all warm and some are still glowing. It was a time for the women to chat amongst themselves, while the priestess prepares for the next part of the ceremony.

'I hear that Bridget is looking after a man at her home,' comments Shannon, a plump witch from the south quarter.

'I heard that the man is from the prison,' stresses Niam, an elderly grey-haired witch, who was the wise woman of the island.

'He is a King, is what I heard,' declares Skatha, a dark-skinned warrior princess, originally from Gaul, but now happily living on Portland.

'I heard that he is a bit of alright,' giggles Morr'igan, rubbing her amethyst, before replacing it into the leather pouch between her breasts.

'Quiet please ladies,' admonishes the priestess, 'We still have work to do.' The witches return to their stations within the circle.

When everyone was settled, Swan Feather holds the athame in front of her.

'I offer my gratitude to that which sustains me. May I always remember the blessings of Nemonta and Nodens.'

She touches the tip of the athame into the jug of mead.

'As the Devine Male joins the Divine Female for the benefit of each other, let the fruits of their Sacred Union promote life, love, and joy. Let the Earth be fruitful, and her bounty be spread throughout the Isle of Portland.'

Swan Feather replaces the athame onto the altar and takes a sip from the jug of mead, tasting the fruitiness as it glides down her throat to her stomach. She passes the jug to Rhiannon on her left. As the mead passes around the circle, the High Priestess touches the dish of oak-cakes with the tip of the athame.

'This food is the blessing that Nemonta and Nodens have given to me. As I have received, may I offer food for the body, mind, and spirit for those that seek it.'

The priestess eats an oak-cake before passing the dish to Rhiannon. When the drink and food offerings return to the North Station, Swan Feather continues her chant.

'As I have enjoyed these gifts of the Goddess and God, may I remember that without them I would be nothing,

So, Mote it Be!'

The coven repeat, 'So Mote it Be.'

Swan Feather holds the athame level over the altar and a thin golden mist showers from the blade to wash over the altar. The athame absorbs the soft yellow steam that rises from the altar.

'Nemonta and Nodens, I have been blessed by you. Thank you for sharing this time with me and my coven, watching over us. We come in love, and we depart in love.'

The priestess raises the athame to the sky. It is time to clear the circle; time to release the forces in the circle. Calling to the universe once more, Swan Feather releases her energy into the fabric of the universe through her voice and words.

'Love is the Law, and the Law is Love. I came in Love I took part in Love, and I leave in Love until we meet again.
This circle is closed.
So, Mote it Be!'

Swan Feather kisses the blade of the athame before she places it back on the altar. The wand is the tool required to send the elementals back to their realms. The priestess thanks each animal spirit in turn before sending them home. The Bear growls and beats his chest as he vanishes into the ether. The Hawk stretches her wings and flies off on a thermal that will take her to the heavens. The Stag raises his head and fades into nothingness and the Otter jumps from the standing stone to disappear in the dark. The circle is notably darker once the elementals have left.

From her North Station facing towards the centre of the circle, the priestess raised her hands, chanting.

'Powers of the visible and invisible depart in peace. You help in my work and whisper in my ear from the Otherworld. Let there always be harmony between us. Take my love with you. The Circle is Cleared.'

The energy and the warmth it gave out dissipates back into the Earth as the coven wait in silence, waiting for Swan Feather to continue. Returning to the physical world, the witches begin to feel the harsh breeze coming in off the sea. The High Priestess signals them to dress and warm themselves. The cloaks give little protection and warmth from the chilly air, even when the witches pull them tight around their shoulders. Swan Feather is beginning to feel tired; it has been a long day. She raises her athame above her head, into the blue halo that borders the circle, and walking anti- sunwise with the blade she draws the energy back into the athame. Back at the altar she touches the tip of the blade against her forehead, causing the blue light to swirl back inside her. The High Priestess raises the athame high chanting.

'The ceremony has ended.'

Moving her arms out to her sides, the priestess continues.

'Blessings have been given.'

She then crosses her arms across her chest,

'And blessings have been received.'

Swan Feather opens her arms towards the circle,

'May the peace of the Goddess and the God remain in my heart.

So, Mote it Be!'

With the ritual over, the priestess lets out a sigh of relief, touching the ground with the palm of her hand to disperse any excess energy and to bring the ceremony to an end.

Of course, Rufus had no idea of what he had just witnessed. What were the flashes of light darting from one place to another inside the circle? Where did the ghostly animal spirits come from, and where did they go? There were many questions forming in Rufus's head. He found the experience a very mystical one—a spiritual journey to the Otherworld and back. It left him feeling warm inside. That warmth was joy; it had been a long while since he had felt joy. Rufus watched as the witches gathered their tools and equipment, whispering and giggling as they left the standing stones circle. Rufus returned quietly to the house.

The fire in the cauldron had almost died out when Rufus returned to the room. He was looking about for wood to burn, to warm him up, when Swan Feather entered. Her cloak was pulled tight around her body. Behind her was the witch Morr'igan, carrying a wicker basket that contained the tools used in the ceremony.

She looked Rufus up and down, admiring his exposed muscular body.

'Hello handsome,' purred Morr'igan. Rufus smiled back and was about to reply when Swan Feather interrupted.

'Thank you Morr'igan. Leave the tools on the table and I will see you tomorrow; sleep well.' Morr'igan put the wicker basket on the table and smiled at Rufus, before turning to Swan Feather and bidding her a good night.

'You should not be up,' spoke Swan Feather, as she strode into one of the darkened rooms to change into something warmer. 'And you certainly should not have seen what you have seen this night,' she called from the darkness. Rufus replied,

'I heard noises and went to see where they were coming from. I do not know where I am or in whose house I sleep. I was curious.'

Returning to the main room, clad in a dress that reached her ankles and a baggy jumper, Swan Feather produced a handful of wood for the fire and ushered Rufus to sit in a chair that she pulled up next to the cauldron. Rufus sat and warmed himself by the fire while Swan Feather got herself a seat and sat opposite.

'I am Bridget,' she revealed, 'a witch of the Luna Order of the Isle, one of several covens on the island.' Rufus had many questions for her,

'I saw the ritual you performed and would like to learn how you produced the light and everything.'

'That ritual was not for your eyes,' Bridget scolded, 'and anyway, most of what you saw was caused by the potion I made to help you recover. It was a very deep wound, and you lost a lot of blood; I had to use a lot of Mandrake in my potion to heal the damage. Mandrake is very toxic and very hallucinogenic.'

The new wood on the fire caught hold, warming, and lighting up the room a bit. Rufus saw that Bridget was a pretty woman of around forty sun cycles old. Her green eyes held him in her presence. 'You have been put into my care until you are fit enough to finish your sentence in the quarries.' Bridget continued, 'Because of your heroic actions, the druids have decided to halve your sentence to four days. You have three and a half days to complete.'

'Wait a minute,' responded Rufus, 'I saved the life of a druid earlier—surely that should revoke the whole sentence?'

'Do you think the druid's life was in danger?' countered Bridget. 'The whole thing was a ploy to find out who was part of the plan to escape. Prisoner 193 was known to us; he was the one who attacked Druid Dalan. The druids were waiting to see who stood by him before taking action. Your heroics put paid to that.'

'I did what I thought best,' argued Rufus; the thought of another three and a half days' work caused him to shudder.

'And the druids respect that; they admire bravery, hence halving your sentence.' Bridget replied, starting to feel tired. 'All this can wait until tomorrow', she tells Rufus, rising to her feet. 'I will get you a concoction to help you sleep.' Tiredness began to tug at Rufus and his wound throbbed.

'Have you anything for my wound?' he asked. 'It is starting to ache.' Bridget left the room to prepare the nightcap. A sprinkle of Burdock root added to the mix of Jasmine, Valerian, and Cowslip should ease his pain. She thought it best not to mention that urine was the main part of the potion.

'Here down this,' she told Rufus, handing him the drink.

'It does not smell very nice,' complained Rufus. 'It is not supposed to.' replied Bridget. 'I am off to my bed; I have a busy day tomorrow. I will be gone by the time you rise. Shannon will come round to see if you are ok in the morning.' Rufus gulped down the nightcap; it tasted better than it smelt. He bid the High Priestess goodnight before finding his way to his bed. A drowsiness overtook him as he slumped onto the bed. He was too tired to undress. Soon his dreams were filtering down into his subconsciousness, dreams that soon turned into nightmares.

TRANSFORMATION

The nightmares had left Rufus when he woke. All he remembered was being chased by hideous demon, like shadows, through a thick forest. Daylight rushed into the room with the easterly breeze blowing in the open doors of the house. A pleasant fragrance flooded his nostrils, causing him to sit up and open his eyes. At first, everything was out of focus in his dimly lit room, but soon his eyes had adjusted to the conditions of his outer reality. His room consisted of the bed he lay on and a chair. Clothes had been put on the chair, not the grey prison uniform, but a fancy set of green flaxen trousers with a brown woollen top. His boots had been cleaned and lined with the fur of an otter or something.

The wound on Rufus's chest hurt when he pulled himself out of his bed. The fine white dressing still covered it and, on the whole, the pain eased once he had dressed and could rest his left arm a little. His first impression of the large room outside his bedroom was the calmness it radiated. It had lilac painted walls, which he had not noticed the night before, and fresh flowers in jugs on the tables. An incense, which smelt like sandalwood smouldered in the cauldron at the centre of the room. Sunlight streamed in through the open door, bringing with it the green smell of spring. Rufus called out to see if anybody was about, but it seemed he was alone in the building. Swan Feather, or rather Bridget, had gone about her duties and Shannon had not yet arrived. A black cat was sleeping on one of the tables. Rufus still felt groggy from his sleep and went into the room that Bridget had brought the drink from the night before. A small room, about the same size as his bedroom, was full of shelves and cabinets, mostly holding vials of liquid and bowls of herbs amongst other strange things. Some scrolls took up one of the shelves.

Rufus needed something for his aching body and dull mind. A vial of animal essence caught his eye. 'That's what I need to perk me up,' he thought, reaching for the orange-coloured liquid in front of him. 'A bit of animal essence will soon have me feeling myself again,' he concluded. He pulled the cork out and gave the potion a good sniff. It smelt ok: like a fresh rose.

'What harm could it do?' he mumbled to himself, before knocking the contents down. A warm feeling grew in his stomach, soon spreading throughout his entire body. Rufus felt good.

Slowly but surely, Rufus became aware of the room growing larger around him. The small vial he held was growing too. What was going on? He put the vial on the floor and realised his clothes had grown and were falling off him. Then it sank in—it was not the room growing, it was him shrinking! Rufus did not stop getting smaller until he was the size of a small rodent. In fact, he was a small rodent: a small plump, grey coney with great long ears and whiskers. Rufus did not like the feeling at all. Maybe he should not have drunk the witch's brew after all. He hopped out of his pile of clothes that surrounded him and slunk into the main room, which by now was massive in size. He noticed the cat was awake and looking menacingly at him from the table. The cat was twice the size that Rufus was. An instinct told him to run, and without another thought Rufus set off as fast as he could run, through the room and out into the open air. He sensed the cat was in hot pursuit, so did not stop once he reached the sunshine and blue skies; he carried on to a thicket of brambles a short distant away. The banshee scream, of the cat echoed in Rufus's long ears, which stretched out behind him as he reached the safety of the spiky brambles and ran down a dark hole into the earth. Rufus stopped running when he felt safe enough, to gather his thoughts. He was a furry rodent; obviously as a result of the potion he had drunk in the witch's house. He was sitting on his haunches in a dark tunnel under the ground. A dark tunnel and yet he could see his way without any light. He knew that the cat was waiting at the entrance of the hole without having to see it; Rufus could sense the danger. He could smell something pleasant further down the dark hole: the aroma of a fresh dandelion leaf. He discerned that there were friendly souls waiting for him at the end of the tunnel; perhaps they could help him out of this predicament so he could become a man again. A munch on the dandelion leaf would help him think. Rufus continued down the tunnel.

Five conies stopped breakfasting on their leaves to stare at Rufus as he entered the roomy cavern. Rufus sat high on his haunches—despite being a coney, he was still a King. He surveyed the room and his new friends. He sensed peace and love, a passionate love! He felt safe.

'I am Rufus and would really like a nibble on one of your lovely fresh leaves,' came Rufus's first response to the situation. Nothing seemed more important than a feast on a succulent leaf at that moment in time.

'Welcome friend, be our guest,' sniffed one of the conies, and ushered Rufus into a space next to him where he could feed. Rufus did not think that a fresh dandelion leaf could be so tasty. He failed to notice the other conies had moved away from the meal and taken positions around Rufus, blocking off any chance of escape. A surge of danger flowed up Rufus's back and he turned to face the circle.

'Brothers,' he pleaded, 'I come in peace and ask for your help.' A large coney took a hop forward towards Rufus,

'Sister, you have come to the right place if you want our help, but first you can help us,' the coney said, finishing with a wicked grin and a long meaningful wink. It took a heartbeat for Rufus to take in what the coney had said: sister? He called me sister; he thinks I am a female.

'Wait my friends,' pleaded Rufus, 'I am not what you think; I am a man. I mean I am a male, not a female.'

'Man? Male? The poor creature does not know what she is,' responded the big coney, with lust in his eyes. 'You are a lady, honey, and we ain't seen a lady around here in a long while,' he added, closing in on Rufus. Rufus leapt at the advancing coney, striking him in the face with her powerful back legs and forcing him back. The lusty coney rubbed his sore nose, anger rising in his blood; nobody hit him in his own home, especially not a lady.

'You might be able to fend off one coney, but you ain't no match for five, lady.' he growled.

Rufus controlled his breathing; he was in for the fight of his life and needed the help of the goddess. His mind cleared and his vision became enhanced. A whisper reverberated from the distance of the universe; it was a soft sound, barely audible even for a coney ear. The whisper floated gently into view. It was a message from the Goddess; it read 'Fireblade.'

Fireblade, Rufus's magic dagger. Was it possible to retrieve Fireblade from the Otherworld as a coney? There was only one way to find out.

Suddenly Fireblade sprang into existence at the centre of the cavern, causing the five conies to bump into each other as they all tried to escape out of the tunnel at once. Rufus sensed their fear and could not help but smile a little. The looks on their faces when Fireblade appeared were so funny.

Rufus called for the conies to come back. The cat still guarded the entrance, so they would not go far.

'I will not hurt you brothers; all I ask is for your help,' he shouted up the tunnel, before returning to the magic dagger. Without hands however, Rufus could not hold Fireblade or send her back to the world of spirit. It would have to remain here for now. Rufus looked down at his paws. 'What use are these?' he mumbled to himself.

'They are used for digging, lady,' spoke the first coney to return to the hole. 'My name is Will, and I am sorry for the way we treated you just then.' Rufus sensed more fear in the coney than sorrow, but he could see the sorrow in his heart and decided not to dwell on the matter.

'I mean you no harm,' Rufus repeated, 'I come here in peace and in need of your assistance.' Will looked down at Fireblade then across to Rufus, sat in a regal pose, her shoulders pushed back, and head held high. 'Do not be afraid Will,' Rufus continued, 'As long as I am not in danger the dagger will remain lifeless. If for any reason things change ...' Rufus left the rest to Will's imagination. The remaining conies one by one slowly returned to their home, their home with a fearful dagger and crazy lady coney that thought she was a man sitting at its centre. They sat in a circle around Rufus, their lustful energies replaced by fear. Some of the fear remained but mostly curiosity filled their heads. They sat in silence waiting for Rufus to speak.

Rufus explained the events that led to her invading their lives: the Oracle, Red Jack, Percival, Lizzy Penn, his arrest on Portland, the hard labour, the heroics that led him to be in the witch's house, the witch's potion, the cat, and the dash for safety. At first the conies were silent, their tiny brains trying to comprehend all the information. Destiny was the first to speak,

'Wasn't it you that hunted and ate two brothers from the Eoaster Tribe on the common?' Rufus could sense the anger rising in their bellies. He took a conscious look towards Fireblade before replying,

'Yes, and I am sorry; I am being punished by the druids in the quarries for that.' Harmony responded before Rufus could continue,

'You think that destroying our habitat entitles you to redemption?' 'How would you like it if your relatives were eaten?' questioned another. The conies rounded on Rufus, 'Why should we believe anything you say? You're just a messed-up lady that belongs with the crazies at the Beale.'

'Stop this,' shouted Will, hopping over to stand next to Rufus. 'What is done, is done,' he resumed when he saw he had their attention.

'She will be judged by the animal spirits when the time comes.' The conies were a little surprised by Will's forwardness, but then, he was the first to return to the crazy situation in the cavern. 'She needs our help, and we need hers.' Will continued, 'Rufus needs to get back into the witch's house and we need to get our ladies back.' A small cheer of agreement came from the conies. Will turned to face Rufus,

'For several moon cycles our ladies have disappeared slowly but surely until they had all gone, hence our excitement and confusion at seeing you. You mentioned Red Jack, no doubt he is the same Lord Jack Belvedore that we believe has been kidnapping our ladies.' Jack Belvedore thought Rufus; he would love to catch up with him. Will continued, 'We will help you get back to the witch's house, and in return when you regain your human body, you must confront Belvedore and return our ladies to us.' A chorus of cheers went around the cavern.

'I agree,' pledged Rufus. 'I entrust you as the guardians of my dagger, Fireblade, until I have fulfilled my promise.' Rufus held out a paw to shake the paw of Will, but that was not the coney way of sealing a pledge. Before she knew it, the conies had surrounded her and began rubbing their fur against hers. It aroused a strange sensation inside Rufus's body: a sense of belonging, a sense of unity, a sense of honour. After a brief discussion, it was decided the best plan to get Rufus back to the house was to create a diversion. It was well-known that there was some bad blood between the cat and Seabhac, the hawk. Will took control of organising the plan. He sent the message to Seabhac to come quickly via the worm spirit, beetle spirit, and the brave wren. Seabhac will soon on his way.

The cat waited patiently at the coney entrance. They feared him, but he would never harm them; he did not want them to know that. Lucifer was supposed to be minding the patient until Shannon arrived, but he was dozing in the morning warmth when the man had drunk the potion and transformed into the coney. He was too slow to realise what was going on before the animal had darted full speed out of the house. The coney was well on its way to the warren before Lucifer was alert enough to leap off the table in hot pursuit. He knew he would be in trouble with Bridget if he lost the man. He was already in trouble for allowing him to steal from the potion cabinet in the first place. He had to get him back before Shannon showed, which was any moment now. Suddenly, he felt the fur on his neck stiffen and turned to see Seabhac swooping towards him. Lucifer leapt out of the way, and then began chasing the hawk into the field of growing crops.

'Now,' yelled Will, pushing Rufus up the tunnel and into the sunshine above ground. Rufus had to blink a few times to allow her eyes to return to daylight mode. Then she saw the witch's house and ran for all she was worth. Twenty coney hops away from the house Rufus tripped on something, leaving her belly down on the grass. When she tried to move, she let out a yelp of pain; she had twisted her ankle and was unable to move. The watching conies held their breath and Lucifer, remembering the man/coney, stopped chasing the hawk and returned to the source of the yelp. Unfortunately for Rufus, a passing fox had heard the coney's sound of distress and was only a gallop away. Sionnach had not eaten in days and nor had her cubs. Fresh coney was on the menu; Rufus was done for. The fox was a breath away when suddenly, hissing and screaming like a banshee, Lucifer flew past Rufus and onto the back of the fox, digging his claws in hard and causing Sionnach to stop in her tracks to try and deal with the crazy cat. The coney could wait. Then Shannon arrived. Sionnach turned and fled, vowing revenge on Lucifer as the cat leapt off her, returning to the peacefulness of the house and his spot in the sun.

The plump witch put down her bag of herbs and broomstick to pick up the poor injured coney. She cradled her between her breasts as she took the injured animal into the sanctuary to tend to her wounds. At least Rufus was safe—for now.

A MAN AGAIN

Inside the sanctuary, Shannon, unaware of his current form placed Rufus carefully onto the table and got a fresh green leaf for the coney to munch on while she searched the building for Rufus. She found a pile of clothes on the floor of the medicine room and tidied them away back into Rufus's room. There was no sign of the man from the mainland.

Rufus relaxed on the table, her heart still beating fast. She was aware of the cat two tables down, sleeping in the sunshine that had come through a slit in the wall, the same cat that had chased her down the coney hole. Rufus had a sniff at the green leaf in front of her, but she had lost her appetite. The ordeal had left her feeling tired, so she opted to have a nap.

When Rufus woke, she was aware of the cat on the table with her, staring at her intently.

'Enjoy your sleep, coney?' Lucifer whispered to Rufus.

'Yes thanks, cat,' replied Rufus, unsure of the cat's intention.

'You were lucky out there you know,' continued Lucifer, that fox would have had you if I had not come to your rescue.' Rufus sat up before replying,

'Thank you for that, but if you had not chased me, I would not have had to run away.'

'If you had not drank the potion, I would not have had to chase you,' Lucifer replied. 'Anyway, my name is Lucifer, I am the witch's cat. You will be in trouble when she returns, for drinking all of her potion.'

'How long will it last?' enquired Rufus.

'I don't know; I am only a cat,' replied Lucifer, 'could be an hour, could be a week.' he concluded, with a big grin.

'It's good you two are getting along,' purred Shannon, as she returned to the room. 'Either of you seen the man?' she enquired, not really expecting an answer from the animals. She did not possess the ability to talk animal, very few people did. She picked Rufus up by the scruff of the neck, cradling her against her breasts with one hand, while feeding her the leaf with the other. Rufus felt obliged to nibble on the leaf. Lucifer leapt off the table and disappeared/ran or similar out of the building in search of adventure.

It was noon when Bridget returned. She had with her Drui'en, her daughter, and was not happy when she saw that her animal potion was gone. It did not take her long to realise what had happened to it. She whispered something to Shannon, who passed Rufus to her, then took Drui'en by the hand and led her into one of the rooms. Bridget held Rufus up in front of her, not revealing that she knew it was Rufus.

'What a nice, plump coney you are,' she told him. 'You will make a nice stew for our dinner tonight.' She smiled, putting the frightened animal into a deep box in the corner of the room. Rufus called out that she was not a coney but a man, but Bridget could only hear coney squeaks coming from the box. She went into the potion room to prepare another concoction of herbs and animal bits.

Rufus was worried. He had to convince the witch who he really was, but how? She tried to call Lucifer, but he had disappeared. She tried to tell Shannon when she came over to put a dish of milk into the box, but she just gave the coney a stroke on the head and licked her lips before disappearing from sight.

After a short time, Drui'en appeared and stroked Rufus gently. The girl was around thirteen cycles old with light brown hair down to her shoulders. A simple green flaxen dress covered her body, leaving her arms and legs bare. She gave Rufus a friendly smile and picked her out of the box, to hold tight in her arms. It was a little too tight for Rufus, squashing her bladder and causing her to wee down the little girl's dress. Drui'en held Rufus away from her when she saw what the coney had done, and with a twist and a scratch, Rufus was free and dropped to the ground. She was not going to be anyone's dinner tonight. Before Rufus had a chance to run, she was swept up by the scruff of the neck by Bridget and held in front of the witch's angry face.

'You are nothing but trouble,' she growled at Rufus, and took him into one of the rooms at the back of the building. Cooking pots and freshly cut vegetables were laid out on a table, a pot of water was heating on a fire at the edge of the room; the smoke rising out of a hole in the roof. Bridget called for Shannon and the plump witch arrived moments later.

'Hold him please,' Bridget told Shannon. 'While I fetch the cutting flint.' Shannon held onto Rufus tight, and Bridget fetched the blade and a handful of herbs. Chanting to the gods and goddesses, Bridget cut and dropped the herbs into the pot of warm water. Rufus was scared and the more she struggled, the tighter Shannon held her. Bridget finished chanting, took hold of Rufus, and plunged him into the pot for a second then placed him on the table, dripping warm water everywhere. Rufus was too shocked to move. Bridget took hold of her wand, raising it to the sky, chanting to the gods and goddesses once again in a language Rufus did not understand. She tapped Rufus on the head three times with her wand, making Rufus's head explode into a thousand dimensions at once, before settling down to the one dimension he knew. His head felt fuzzy as he tried to focus on his surroundings. He saw the two witches looking at him, grinning at him. He was aware of his body; his naked, human body sat on the table. He was back; he was a man again and he was happy. Then he remembered he was naked and tried to cover himself with his hands. The witches laughed and Shannon went to collect his clothes for him.

Rufus still felt a little strange when he was dressed and was given a hot potion to drink that Bridget had made. It was very bitter.

'That will help you recover.' Bridget told him. 'The effects of the animal essence will take a while to leave your body; there will be some side effects for a time.'

'What kind of side effects?' Rufus queried. Bridget just waved her hands and ignored the question. She wanted him to know the trouble he had caused with his stupidity. Rufus was not used to being admonished but he did deserve his telling off. She told him the potion that he had used up turned people into their inner animal.

'But my inner animal is the bear,' Rufus insisted.

'If your inner animal is the bear,' Bridget replied, 'then you would have turned into a bear, not a coney.'

Bridget replaced the dressing on Rufus's chest and invited him outside, to sit in the sunshine with Shannon and Drui'en.

A cool breeze swept up over the island, encouraging seagulls to hover on the thermals overhead. Rufus tucked into the bread and cold meat and salad from the table outside the witch's sanctuary. Rufus helped himself to the fresh jug of spring water to quench his thirst. The spring sun felt warm on his skin, helping Rufus to relax a little.

'Your daughter Drui'en does not say much,' remarked Rufus, watching the child quietly nibble on a piece of bread.

'She cannot talk,' explained Bridget. 'She has been struck dumb ever since her father was carried away by a sea dragon, nearly a cycle ago.' she told Rufus.

'A sea dragon?' remarked Rufus, 'I thought they died out many cycles ago. I have not heard of a sighting of a dragon of any kind for many cycles.'

'Neither had we on Portland, until that morning of the last spring equinox.' replied Bridget. 'The dragon appeared suddenly, dragging Tom from his fishing boat before disappearing into the mist that shrouded the island that morning. We have not seen anything of him since. It is Tom's clothes that you are wearing,' she added. Shannon put her hand on Bridget's arm to console her. She knew the agony the High Priestess was going through.

'I'm sure your husband will return one day,' she tried to reassure her friend. 'The Prophetess Fedel'ma says he is still alive, somewhere outside of space and time.' After a brief silence around the table Bridget continued,

'Since that day, the trauma has caused Drui'en to be mute. She has not spoken a word, despite being seen by the top druids and subjected to a myriad of witches' spells.'

'I am sorry.' Rufus responded, putting his hand on Bridget's shoulder. Drui'en leapt up and threw her arms around her mother.

Suddenly a voice echoed in Rufus's mind,

'Hey human, don't forget about us.' Rufus looked around to see where the voice was coming from. In the bushes next to the sanctuary Rufus could see a coney in the shadows; it looked like Will. 'Don't forget our deal, human. We helped you return to the witch's house, now help return our ladies,' the voice continued. Rufus was definitely hearing it inside his head. The sensation made him sit bolt upright, causing Bridget and Shannon to stare at him.

'What's the matter?' queried Bridget. Rufus regained his composure quickly.

'When I was in the coney warren, they told me Jack Belvedore has been stealing the female conies and selling their fur and paws as lucky charms on the mainland. All of their ladies have disappeared, leaving them frustrated and angry.' Bridget was shocked to hear this.

'It makes sense,' she said. 'The druids are aware of the coney population diminishing; that is why they were so harsh in sentencing you for eating two of them.' she added, standing. 'I must report it to the Archdruid at once.'

Rufus helped the witches pack the food back into the house.

'I needed to replace the mandrake this afternoon.' Bridget announced, while they worked. 'Mandrake was the main ingredient of the potion you drank this morning.' she barked, turning to Rufus. 'Take my daughter with you to the Beale; she knows where the mandrake grows. I will try and quash your conviction with the Archdruid because of your help; but I need that mandrake today.' Turning to Shannon, Bridget told her to gather the sisters to meet back at the sanctuary at sunset. Bridget rushed off, leaving Shannon to prepare Drui'en for the walk to the infirmary at the Beale. She put sturdy walking boots on her and a red cape to protect her from the harsh winds that always raged at the south of the island. She found a brown woollen cloak for Rufus to wear. Drui'en ran into her room to collect her wicker basket that she used to gather herbs from around the island. She loved to gather herbs for her mother and her friends.

TO THE BEALE

Spring blooms were beginning to carpet the island, with their bright yellow and pink petals swaying in the south-westerly breeze. The fresh smell of nature invaded Rufus's nostrils as he and Drui'en started their trek along the eastern side of the island. The well-trodden path wound its way south along the steep cliffs. Copses of elms gave sporadic shade from the early afternoon sun as Rufus and Drui'en walked silently towards the Beale. Rufus listened to the waves gently crashing onto the rocks below, and a warm breeze from across the island bathed his skin. He felt at peace with himself and stopped to experience the world around him for a few moments. Energy from the universe entered his inner being, enriching his soul. He took a few long breaths before returning to his mission to collect mandrake for the witch. Looking down at Drui'en, he saw that she was holding a snake; the black diamond shapes down its back told Rufus it was a poisonous snake. He instructed Drui'en to put the snake down slowly.

'I won't bite her, you fool,' the snake replied, giving Rufus a jolt. 'Me and Drui'en often have chats when our paths meet; she is a very intelligent girl.'

'You can communicate with the girl?' enquired Rufus, still coming to terms with being able to speak with the animals. One of the side effects Bridget told him about, Rufus suspected.

'What does she say?' he asked.

'She, says many things, like all children do. She loves her mum and misses her dad. And she thinks you are funny.'

'Funny? Me?' Rufus responded, unsure if that was a good thing or bad thing.

'Anyway Rufus, the day draws on and I have much to do before the sun sets. My name is Nathair, and it was a pleasure to meet you.'

'My pleasure.' replied Rufus, as Drui'en gently putting Nathair into the grass.

'One more thing before I go,' called the snake, 'If you get the chance, it would be beneficial to call in on old Pellinore at the Infirmary while you are there.' Rufus thanked Nathair as the snake slithered away, up towards the Grove. Rufus looked at Drui'en hard,

'So, you think I am funny, do you?' he questioned, raising his eyebrows. Drui'en looked at Rufus in all innocence then, unable to hide her feelings, began to giggle and laugh, which made Rufus laugh as well. Together they laughed, which made the universe and everything in it seem a better place to be.

In a valley just past a lookout tower, Rufus and Drui'en could see a stone temple; it was next to a pond, overlooking an accessible sandy cove.

'I would not mind having a look at that temple; we have plenty of time.' declared Rufus. Drui'en nodded her agreement and the pair skirted down the slope towards the temple.

The whiteness of the temple radiated light from the sun, bringing a sparkle to the pond. A small streamlet snaked its way down the small valley and over a ledge to feed the pond, with the overspill flowing out over the cliff to the beach below and out to sea. The temple itself was about five paces square with a roof on pillars. A waist-high wall a further two paces out surrounded the holy place. A statue of a Goddess facing out to sea stood at the centre of the shrine.

'What Goddess is that?' Rufus queried, turning to the girl, and forgetting Drui'en could not respond. Drui'en smiled back and pointed to a raven that had swooped down to roost on a branch of one of the few small oaks that were growing nearby. Rufus looked over to the bird,

'Hey bird, do you know who the Goddess is?' he called. The raven looked back at Rufus and waited a few moments before replying,

'I am a raven, and my name is Bran,' and then turned away again. Rufus looked down at Drui'en who gestured that he should ask the raven again, but more politely. Rufus turned towards the raven,

'Good day Bran, my name is Rufus. Do you happen to know who the Goddess in the temple is?' Bran replied,

'Yes.' Rufus glanced back at Drui'en, taking a deep breath before returning his focus to the bird.

'Please Bran, could you tell me the name of the Goddess that is worshipped here?' Bran glided from his branch, swooped over the pond and with a single flap of his wings, rose to perch on the top of the temple.

'The Goddess is Belisama, the Goddess of Light and the Fire, who crafts and forges the newly discovered metals.' Metal was a recent discovery to Albion, coming in from the east like so many new ideas, and reaching these shores through trade and travel. Bronze was the easiest to melt and cast into tools and weapons, but tin and gold were also being found and worked locally.

'There are two cast gold cats that are used to adorn the temple on special occasions,' continued Bran.

Golden cats, thought Rufus, "Golden cats in temples of stone, the spell of time is your friend." He knew he was on the right track.

Drui'en tugged at Rufus's cloak, indicating they had to go. Rufus nodded his agreement.

'Well thank you for your help Bran. We have to go now. It was nice to have met you.'

'Before you go,' spoke Bran, giving his wings a flap, 'Old Pellinore likes Lady's Mantle, if by any chance you see him. He would be very grateful you know.' And before Rufus could respond, the raven took off and flew north towards the Verne Hill.

'Thanks,' called Rufus as Bran disappeared out of view. He turned to Drui'en, shrugging his shoulders, 'Lady's Mantle?' Drui'en giggled and pulled Rufus away from the temple and up the other side of the valley.

A couple of wispy white clouds drifted across the sky as the pair continued their walk to the Beale. Rufus bade each animal he saw a good afternoon, which made Drui'en giggle to herself each time. Soon they had reached Sandholes and crossed the small bridge over the river that flowed down from Culverwell and left the island as a waterfall, crashing into the sea below. Drui'en stopped and began to search in the short grass next to the cliff for the tiny yellow-headed plant her mother used for medicinal potions: Lady's Mantle. She filled a quarter of her basket with the plant, giving each one a blessing in her head before cutting them with a flint blade. She was more armed than Rufus was, but even without a weapon he still felt safe. There was something special about the process of gathering the foliage. Each cutting felt special and was happy to give their service to Drui'en.

From this point, Rufus could see down to the most southern tip of the island. He noticed the wind felt much stronger and wilder now that he was exposed to the full force of it coming in from the channel. He could also see the stockade-like structure of the Infirmary, the world of the mad, thought Rufus. Once Drui'en had thanked the plant spirits for their gift, she held Rufus's hand and walked him on.

In a hollow, out of the wind, and near to the Infirmary walls, Drui'en knelt over a mandrake and was talking to it in her head. She put her hands gently around the stem and sent it love from her heart. The mandrake released its hold on the earth and offered itself to the girl. Drui'en pulled it gently from the ground, kissed it, thought a small prayer, and thanked the earth spirits for their kindness. After placing three mandrake plants into her basket, each one having their own individual ceremony, Drui'en thanked the hollow in the ground, and then thanked the earth herself.

'I guess while we are here, we might as well call in to see if Lizzy and Percival are about,' said Rufus, looking at Drui'en as if he needed her approval. Drui'en shrugged her shoulders, as if to say she did not mind. The height of the Infirmary walls was twice as tall as Rufus. He knocked hard on a sliding panel in a door and after a time, it opened to reveal the face of a tough-looking man.

'Hello sir,' greeted Rufus, 'I would like to see my friends, Lizzy Penn and Percival, if it is not too much trouble.' He attempted a feeble smile at the man.

The face looked down at Drui'en and welcomed her,

'Hello, Drui'en my dear, it is always a pleasure to see you. Come on in, both of you.' He slammed the panel shut and opened the door for the two visitors. The Infirmary was not at all what Rufus was expecting inside: there were no buildings to house the inmates, only wilderness. A rocky wasteland plateau of stone with massive deep cracks radiating out towards the sea and not much else. Rufus and Drui'en were soon surrounded by curious eyes. Several of the inmates, dressed in dirty robes, which made them look like reject monks, came to greet Drui'en and wonder about Rufus. The man who had let them in whispered something to a young woman, who ran off into one of the chasms in the ground.

'I have sent for both Lizzy and Percival; feel free to wander about while you wait.' Rufus noticed that the tall wooden wall did not even surround the enclosure completely; the cliff edge was open to the outside world and all the elemental forces that blew in from the south.

Lizzy was the first to arrive and she seemed happy to see Rufus. He was not sure how much trouble he had got her into. In fact, Lizzy was pleased to see Rufus, and was always pleased to see Drui'en. The witch's daughter spent a lot of time at the Infirmary. She seemed to have a way with the patients, and they liked her. Rufus caught up on all the activities that had gone on since they last saw each other. Lizzy had heard of the fight in the Star Inn and found out about his arrest later. She was called to answer to Druid Caledinn about her association with Rufus and Percival. Because she could answer for Percival, he got sent to her here. She did not know anything about Rufus, only that he claimed that he was a King and wanted to do business on the island. They could not understand why a King would disguise himself as a trader to visit the island. She could not answer that. She heard Rufus had got eight days of hard labour and was then injured during an escape attempt.

'It was not me that was trying to escape,' exclaimed Rufus quickly, 'I saved a druid's life from someone trying to escape,' he explained, putting the story straight.

Then Percival arrived at the reunion.

'Hey, Rufus, good to see yer, my friend,' and he hugged Rufus tightly.

'Good to see you too Percival,' Rufus replied. The three caught up on recent events. It seemed all three were feeling good in themselves at that moment. Rufus suddenly remembered Pellinore and asked if he was on duty. Drui'en started to giggle while Lizzy looked at Rufus in horror.

'Pellinore does not work here, he is a patient,' she enlightened him.

'I would still like to see him,' Rufus asked.

'That man is as crazy as craziness gets; Pellinore does not have any sort of contact with anyone if he can help it.' Lizzy responded.

'Still, I would like to see him.' Rufus pleaded.

'Be my guest,' Lizzy retorted, 'If he does not want to be seen, he will not be found.'

Drui'en removed the mandrakes from the basket and wrapped them in her cloak, before passing the basket of Lady's Mantle to Rufus.

'You want me to come with you?' offered Percival.

'No thanks,' Rufus replied, 'I will be ok.'

He set off past the caverns and out towards the open cliffs, to the place Lizzy had shown him, where Pellinore might be found. At the cliff edge Rufus called out Pellinore's name. The wind was fierce, and Rufus had to hold the plants in the basket down to stop them blowing away.

'I have some Lady's Mantle for you, and I would like to speak to you.' he called to the wind. Large caves could be seen in the cliff face around towards the northern wall, but the path to them looked hazardous and was crumbling into the sea.

Rufus was just about to give up when he became aware of a figure watching him from behind. He turned to look at the skeletal man that faced him. Dressed only in a filthy rag around his waist and offering a toothless grin, crouched Pellinore.

'I was once like you,' the ragged man snarled, 'I too was once a powerful King; then she came.' Pellinore lowered his head to the ground.

'Who came?' questioned Rufus, 'And how do you know I am a King?'

'Who she is, is not important,' answered Pellinore, 'and neither is how I know you are a King. I know everything; that is the curse that imprisons me here. I knew you were coming! You have something for me?' he growled. Rufus passed him the basket of Lady's Mantle. Pellinore sniffed at them and rubbed them, took a bite from one and crushed one in his hands.

'Quality gear, from the fair hands of Drui'en I see.' Pellinore disclosed. 'You wanted to speak to me?' asked the old man, his long grey hair falling over the front of his face.

'A snake told me it would be beneficial for me to seek you out,' answered Rufus as honestly as he could, even if it did not sound right.

'Ah, I see you have met Nathair; he is a good creature to have at your side in times of trouble.' informed Pellinore. He stared into Rufus's eyes, reaching out, towards the door to his soul. What he wanted to tell him would affect the lives of the people of Portland. It commanded Rufus's full attention.

'What I tell you goes no further than us; do you understand?' Pellinore began. Rufus nodded. The old man left a lengthy silence before divulging his knowledge to the King. 'For nearly a cycle Druid Balise has been ... how can I say this? He enchanted Drui'en into silence to keep her from telling anyone how he has been abusing her regularly. And it was Balise that summoned up the sea dragon to carry away her father as a further guarantee of her silence. As long as she was quiet, her father lived.' Rufus was speechless. His first reaction was to storm up to the druid and confront him then give him a good hiding. Pellinore called his attention back, 'There is nothing you can do; there is nothing anyone on this island can do. Balise is the most powerful druid on the island by far.'

'Then why tell me?' questioned Rufus. 'What can I do?'

'You are a King; a King by blood, a King initiated by the Goddess.' Pellinore waited a few heartbeats for it to sink in. 'There is one person that is more powerful than Balise, who will blast his fat ass into the Underworld. We need you to fetch her.'

'Fetch who from where?' Rufus queried, 'This has to be stopped now; where is this person?' he demanded. Pellinore waited for Rufus to calm down before continuing. 'She is Eoaster, daughter of the moon goddess,

Nemonta. She is capable of great love but be warned, she is very vengeful when slighted; she can be easily aroused into a terrifying anger.'

'I will get her,' pledged Rufus, 'Where is she?'

'Eoaster dwells with the dead souls in the Underworld. She retired there after getting tired of humans causing death and suffering to each other, and to the earth spirit too. She left this realm a long time ago, to allow humanity to find its own way within the creation of the universe. To fetch her you will need to enter the realm of the Underworld. Tomorrow morning is the last full moon, and when the red Goddess, descends towards the western horizon, you must enter Cruachan's Cave. It is the mouth of the Underworld and your entrance to seek, find, and persuade Eoaster to return. It won't be easy.' It was clear to Rufus what he had to do. He had time to retrieve Fireblade from the conies and get some well-earned sleep before his journey. He told Pellinore he would return in the morning and fetch the retired Goddess. Pellinore handed back the empty basket to Rufus and thanked him for the flowers.

The sun was sauntering down into the western skies; Rufus and Drui'en would be lucky to get back to the Sanctuary before sunset. They said their goodbyes to Lizzy and Percival, but not before Rufus whispered to the hobgoblin his plan to return early in the morning and to be on the lookout for him.

Rufus wondered if Drui'en knew that he knew what was happening to her. She gave no indication of knowing; she just kept looking at him and grinning. They walked back at a quick pace, reaching home some time before the sun set, and just as the first of Bridget's coven were arriving.

INTO THE UNDERWORLD

Shannon got Drui'en washed and clean. She was now old enough to sit in on coven meetings, but Rufus was not allowed. First and foremost, he wasn't a woman; he also wasn't an Islander or a witch; therefore, he needed to be entertained elsewhere. Morr'igan and Bridget had already discussed the threat of a war party from across the channel, especially now the Prophetess had said an attack was imminent. The witches had to be ready. The druids were preparing their battle staffs and wands, but they believed the threat was a while away yet. No one would attack on a waning moon and risk the adverse influence of the Black Goddess in her guise of the Crone. It was a time of conclusion, not renewal, and certainly not a good time for war. No, the druids believed that there would be no threat until at least the summer solstice. Morr'igan was pretty much up to date with the events, so was chosen to take Rufus to witness the sunset. She liked that idea.

Rufus meanwhile was trying to negotiate the return of Fireblade from the conies,

'Look, I know your ladies have not yet been returned, but things are in motion.' Bridget had filled in Rufus on her visit to the Archdruid about Lord Belvedore kidnapping the female conies. Belvedore was away from the island at the moment and Cathbad wanted to wait until he arrived back before taking any action. Bridget had persuaded him to send men to have a look around his farm in East town tomorrow. Rufus explained to the conies that the ladies would be found, and they would return home, but that he needed his dagger now.

'You have to trust me,' begged Rufus.

'Why can't you wait until tomorrow?' queried Will, 'That was the deal.'

'I know,' agreed Rufus, 'but early tomorrow I begin a quest of the utmost importance. I cannot tell you what it is, but it does concern the wellbeing of Portland and everything on the island. I need Fireblade to help me succeed.' he pleaded. After a short discussion, the conies agreed to return the dagger. It sat in their home like a curse anyway, they would be glad to be rid of it if they were honest.

At that moment Morr'igan came out of the house, looking to take Rufus to Tout Dolmen to watch the sunset. Seeing him nearby, she began walking towards him.

'Look, have the dagger waiting for me here at the predawn chorus. I have to go.' Rufus turned to Morr'igan just as she reached him.

'Talking to the brambles, were you?' and she laughed, putting her arm on his. 'Bridget asked me to show you our oldest dolmen on the island and watch the sunset at the same time;

it is not far.' Rufus would have rather had an early night because tomorrow was going to be a busy day, but he knew an important meeting was being held in the Sanctuary, so he agreed to walk with the witch. In a short time, the pair had reached the dolmen overlooking the west cliffs. The great bank of pebbles stretched far into the distance, separated from the mainland by the tidal fleet.

'This is a nice place to sit,' encouraged Morr'igan, pointing to a soft patch of grass near to the cliff edge. Rufus was mesmerised by the multi-coloured sky as the sun dropped towards the sea. When both were sitting comfortably, Morr'igan revealed from her cloak a bay leaf and handed it to Rufus.

'Chew on this and enjoy the moment.' The witch took a bay leaf for herself and put it in her mouth, encouraging Rufus to do the same. It had a pleasant taste to it thought Rufus, trying to relax after an extraordinarily strange day that had ended in an unquenchable rage towards Balise. He was also worried about entering the Underworld the following day, facing an aggressive goddess, and hopefully returning unharmed. Morr'igan pulled herself close to Rufus, telling him to leave his thoughts behind and enjoy her company. A sunset was a miracle of the Sun God Belenus. Rufus cleared his mind the best he could and focused on the altar of Zeus descending towards the Underworld. It was the orange and pink sky that followed the sun on its way down that flowed into his consciousness, dispelling any lingering negative thoughts. The lower the sun dropped, the more vivid the sky. Rufus watched the Earth's great star hit the surface of the water and slowly sink out of view.

Suddenly an arm held Rufus's shoulder and gently pulled him to the ground. It belonged to Morr'igan. Rufus did not put up much of a struggle, and less so when she climbed on top of him. Before he knew it, her lips were on his; then her tongue began to caress the inside of his mouth. Rufus responded, releasing a pent-up energy; passion shot up through his spine to explode in his senses. As the last sparkle of the sun disappeared into the night and the stars began to shine in the heavens, Morr'igan began to undress.

Will was not impressed at all. The coney had followed Rufus and Morr'igan to Tout Dolmen. He would have thought that Rufus would be preparing better for his descent into the Underworld in the morning. His brothers, with the help of the stoats, fabricated from ivy twine a harness for the magic dagger. Now it was just a case of dragging it to the surface for the predawn chorus. Will took a last look at the couple, now both naked and caressing passionately. He wished Rufus the best of luck and hopped home to see how his brothers were getting on.

～⌒～✕～⌒～

A little bird told Rufus it was time to wake up. A wagtail perched on his chest and gave it a peck. Rufus's eyes flickered open.

'Come on, get up man,' the wagtail chirped, rousing Rufus half-way to full attention.

'Are you the predawn chorus?' Rufus mumbled, trying to focus on the little bird in the dim light.

'No, I am the pre-predawn chorus. The conies are waiting with your dagger; it is time to go.' Rufus sat up, causing the wagtail to flutter down to the floor.

'Let the conies know I am coming,' instructed Rufus, fumbling for his clothes. The wagtail took off to pass the message on, a little hurt the human had not thanked him, but then again, the man would probably be dead by sundown. Only Gods, Goddesses, and demi-gods ever returned from the Underworld. The poor man had a lot on his plate.

The fluttering of wings woke Lucifer, his cat radar switched on even when he slept. A bird in the house? he thought, shaking himself awake, most unusual. Lucifer calmly left the comfort of Drui'en's dirty clothes to investigate the strange occurrence at this early time. He saw the small bird fly into Rufus's room and curiosity got the better of him; he silently made his way to the room. He watched the two conversing and Rufus stumbling in the dark to dress. *And those damned conies are in on this mystery as well, are they?* fumed the cat. He crept back into the dark shadow of night and waited.

The chilled night air wrapped her arms around Rufus as he left the Sanctuary. The large waning moon hovered gracefully in the heavens and her attendants, the stars, sparkled as they accompanied their queen across the skies. Rufus looked at her, acknowledged her presence, and asked for her blessing. Without his knowing, Nemonta heard the plea and looked down to see where it came from. She recognized the man as the spy at one of the full moon ceremonies; *which one?* Then she remembered, *the Luna Order of the Isle at the Grove Stones. What has brought him here?* The Moon Goddess decided to pay a little more attention to the man; a man who calls himself King yet wanders the land in poor man's clothes.

The conies wished Rufus good luck while he returned Fireblade to the Otherworld.

'I hope to see you all again before sundown,' Rufus said, clearing his mind ready for the task ahead. He added 'And I expect to find you reunited with your ladies,' before turning towards his destiny. He wrapped his cloak tight around himself and headed into the darkness.

The night was darker than Rufus had expected, despite the moon only just passing her fullness. She shone bright in the south-western sky, but her radiance failed to find her way to Portland. Rufus stumbled down the dark path towards the Beale, tripping over every hidden obstacle on the way. He was aware of the steep cliff to his left and kept a fair distance from that, but the path that was so easy to walk the last evening was completely different in the dark. Every dip and mound, every stone and boulder in the ground, took it in turns to meet the King's walk.

'You having trouble, man?' a deep voice called from Rufus's right.

'What? Who are you?' called Rufus, wondering what sort of animal he was speaking with now.

'I am Styx the owl,' came the reply.

'You look like you need help.'

'Why is it so dark, despite the moon bright in the sky?' asked Rufus.

'A thin veil has been enchanted over the island, deflecting the moon's energy,' explained the owl. 'It is an ingredient of another event quite apart from yours, that is also happening at this moment. Unfortunately for you, that action is affecting your journey.'

'Witch magic,' cursed Rufus.

'No, not witch magic,' explained Styx. 'The magic is from across the channel, to prevent the Goddess energy from reaching the witch ceremonies that will soon be starting all over the island.'

'I have to reach the Beale before sunrise,' declared Rufus, 'and I will never get there before sunrise at this rate,' he complained.

'You could ask your accomplice to lead the way,' argued the owl; cats are very capable of seeing in the dark.'

'What! I do not have an accomplice,' argued Rufus, 'I am all alone.'

'No, you are not,' Styx claimed. 'You have been followed ever since you left the witch's house, followed by her cat.' Rufus looked around in the darkness for the animal, but the cat remained invisible. 'Lucifer, come out now,' demanded Styx, forcing the cat to curse the bird, and come out into the open.

'Damn you owl,' screeched Lucifer, 'can't you mind your own business for once?' Rufus could just about make out Lucifer in the darkness in front of him and waited for an explanation.

'I saw you talking to the bird in your room, then I found out the conies were involved with whatever you were up to, so I followed you,' Lucifer declared. The cat waited for an answer from Rufus.

'I am going to the Beale,' said Rufus hesitantly, unable to decide how much to tell

Lucifer. What the Hades! He was only a cat; it would not change anything if he knew and anyway, he needed Lucifer's help along the dark path to the Beale.

'I will tell you as we walk if you will guide me to the Infirmary; I need to be there before the sun rises,' Rufus revealed. Lucifer thought a while before agreeing. Rufus had acted suspiciously ever since he arrived on the Isle of Portland and he wanted to know what was going on, especially since the conies knew something. Lucifer had to be in the loop too. They carried on south, with Lucifer leading and Rufus following. It did not help much that Lucifer was black, but Rufus could just make out his movements in the darkness as they made their way slowly southwards.

'You're going to fetch Eoaster from the Underworld?' screeched Lucifer, stopping dead in his tracks. 'Are you crazy? You need placing in the Infirmary,' argued the cat.

'The entrance is in the Infirmary,' confirmed Rufus, ignoring the insults. 'The Druid Balise has proved to be an enemy of Portland, and only the Goddess can conquer him.'

That would be a great battle to witness, thought Lucifer, now warming to Rufus.

'What is the coney's part in all this?' queried Lucifer.

'They guarded my magic dagger when it had to be hidden,' answered Rufus, quite at ease in speaking to animals now. He hoped the side-effect lasted a while yet. It had proved to be very helpful. Lucifer decided that he wanted to be a part of the adventure; if the conies were a part of the plot, and quite possibly the fox and the hawk, then he should be too. It seemed everyone knew about this except him.

Soon they were going past the temple that radiated the light of the moon, lighting up the whole of the basin that sat in between the old village of Wake Hamlet and the beach. The temple seemed to be able to penetrate the enchanted veil. Rufus felt the lure of the shrine calling him down. Lucifer knew what he was going to do but didn't try and stop him; it was his destiny after all. He followed Rufus down the valley slope.

At the temple, Rufus calmed the thoughts and feelings that had been racing around his head and called to the Goddess.

'Dear Goddess, Belisama, receiver of the Moon's light and energy on this auspicious and enchanted morning, I offer my services to your cause if only you could pass on some of that light to me in mine.' After a long period of silence from the Goddess, Rufus stood away from the temple in disappointment, not that he had really expected anything. The Goddess had no reason to listen to someone who had only heard of her existence the day before.

'It was worth a go,' consoled Lucifer, his enthusiasm fuelling his adventurous spirit.

Over the valley bank, Portland spread out before Rufus, bathed in the soft silver light of the moon, free of the magic filter from overseas.

'Thank you, Belisama,' Rufus whispered, upping his pace now he could see clearly where he was going. Lucifer had to run to keep up.

Nemonta was not upset that Rufus believed it was Belisama's help he received. The Goddess of the forge was not strong enough against the warlock magic to help Rufus, but it was through Belisama that Nemonta connected with him. It was not long before Rufus and Lucifer were striding up to the gates of the Infirmary.

CRUACHAN'S CAVE

Anxiety began to fill Rufus's mind as he lightly tapped the sliding panel. He was surprised when the panel slid back to reveal the face of the tough- looking man and not Percival. The man simply slid the panel back and unlocked the door to let Rufus in, followed closely behind by Lucifer. The doorkeeper had not been expecting a cat but nonetheless allowed him to enter the Infirmary, before closing the door. Inside the walls Lizzy and Percival waited.

Some secret mission this is, thought Rufus as he hugged Lizzy and slapped Percival on his shoulder.

'What is going on?' demanded an agitated Rufus. 'Why are you here? Did you tell Lizzy, Percival?' It was the doorkeeper that replied,

'Not much that goes on round 'ere gets past me. T'was the patients themselves that told me you were coming this early morn. You are welcome.' He looked down at Lucifer,

'I didn't know about you, but you too are welcome. A witch's cat is always a good omen.' Rufus calmed himself. The day was beginning to shift the night from the land. The sun himself would be rising into the heavens soon. The bright moon shone over the western horizon giving Rufus some confidence and reducing some of his fear, and a strong wind swept in from the sea bringing with it a chill to the air. He had to find Pellinore. Rufus turned towards his friends,

'I must go,' he told them and turned to find the old skeletal man at the cliff edge. He stopped after several paces, realising he was being followed, and turned to find Percival and Lucifer behind him.

'I'm coming too,' notified Percival. Lucifer, seeing the hobgoblin stride after Rufus, followed behind. If the hobgoblin is going, he was going too.

'Go back, both of you,' ordered Rufus. 'This is my responsibility; the pair of you have been a great help in my quest already and I thank you. However, there is a good chance that it will be a one-way journey so if you value your lives, stay here.'

'Rufus,' Percival began, 'I am your friend. My adventure began in the Meadow of Delights days ago and accompanying you to the Underworld is all I ask: to be by your side when you face death.' Rufus refused his request,

'No, I do not want you to get hurt. Stay here!' Rufus continued to walk towards the sea only to find that Percival and Lucifer were still following.

'I am coming with you whether you like it or not,' demanded Percival. Lucifer was going so he could be one up on the conies, and the fox and the hawk. Lucifer was going to be the King of the Grove animals when he returned.

The Underworld held no fear for him; he still had six of his nine lives left.

Rufus did not have time to argue, it was up to them if they wanted to come with him. He strode towards the old man. The patients in the Infirmary began to appear from the shadows as the day got lighter, lining the path to Pellinore. Then they began to quietly chant his name, and then a few called the name of Percival, and even Lucifer was spoken once or twice in the adulation.

'Welcome Rufus and friends,' called Pellinore as the trio approached. The three nodded back, none felt very vocal at that moment. Pellinore handed Rufus a bronze pendant on a length of cord. 'This will guarantee your journey across the dark river to the gates of the Underworld. Then it will be up to you to get past the three dogs that guard the entrance.

Dogs, thought Lucifer, no one said anything about dogs.

'Remember one thing,' continued Pellinore, 'Once inside you must never speak to any dead souls that you meet. Once you utter a single word to the dead, you too are dead and will be unable to leave the realm.' Rufus glanced at the metal symbol for a second before putting it into his cloak pocket. It was like nothing he had seen before. Rufus pictured the face of Balise in his mind and his determination and confidence rose. He looked at Percival and

Lucifer and gave them an unconvincing smile, before following Pellinore to the crumbling path and cliffs he had noticed the day before. Pellinore nimbly danced across to the caves, but Rufus and Percival took great care and time negotiating the dangerous wind-buffeted and slippery route. Lucifer, bringing up the rear, did not know what the fuss was about. He was more worried about the dogs.

A large, narrow, but tall slit in the cliffs welcomed the group. A dark tunnel led inland. Pellinore wished them all luck before chanting to the Moon Goddess as she began her descent into the sea. Her consort, the sun, was only moments away from arriving in the mortal world, as the trio began their walk into the depths of the earth. It reminded Rufus of when he was in the coney hole, and he felt his coney instincts kick in. Like, when he could see his way around the cavern without light, and now (or how), he could see his way in the tunnel just the same. He saw that Percival and Lucifer had no trouble navigating the tunnel without light, but then they had good dark vision anyway. Rufus was sure he could sense the Goddess too or was it his imagination? A sweet smell had drifted into his consciousness, not the smell of a fresh leaf, but a more aromatic rose petal kind of smell. How a goddess would smell, thought Rufus and marched on.

After a short time, they arrived at the entrance to a large chamber lit up with fire spewing out of cracks in the rock walls. At the far end, the trio could see Cruachan's Cave: the entrance to the Underworld and two of the dogs that guarded it. The fur on Lucifer's back rose and his claws flicked out from his paws; he was on full alert. A dark, slow-flowing river separated them from the other side. Across the river a large plateau awaited them that led up to the realm of the dead. First, they had to cross the river. 'You have to call the ferryman,' a large black spider called from his web, hanging from the roof of the cave. 'His name is Charon, and he will come for the caller of his name.'

Is there no animal that I cannot not speak with? Will I be expected to bid a good morning to every beast, bird, or insect that I meet, he mused, while peering up and down the river. He thanked the spider silently then called out to Charon the ferryman.

'Charon, I require your services. I ask you to come to my assistance.' A silent draught echoed down the river. Rufus called again, 'Charon, I bring with me a gift so that you will transport me and my friends safely across the river to Cruachan's Cave.' For a few heartbeats only silence called out to Rufus and then a horn blast chased the silence down river. Charon had heard and was on his way. Soon a mist appeared from upriver, and its vapour transported the ferryman towards Rufus.

Charon appearing from the mist as he came towards them made the three travellers' shudder as the ferry came to a stop beside them. The tall, black-robed ferryman held out a skeletal hand towards Rufus, wanting payment. Rufus handed Charon the pendant that Pellinore had given them.

'It is for a return journey,' informed Percival.

'And for three,' confirmed Lucifer. Charon looked intensely at all three creatures in front of him, his face hidden in the shadows of his hood. Fear reached into the souls of the trio, tearing into their unconscious in a search for their true selves. Charon looked at his fare and placed it in a pouch around his neck. Fear retreated from the travellers and back into the hidden eyes of the ferryman.

'Get in,' Charon growled, 'and no talking.'

In the small wooden boat, propelled by a single oar at the back, Rufus, Percival, and Lucifer were each engaged with the river demons. They were their own personal demons that dwelt in the dark shadows of their minds: the demons of death, of failure, of guilt, and hurt, to name a few. They came, harassing and mocking their weaker minds. And for Lucifer, it was the demon of dogs chasing him all around his universe. The heat and noise of the fires grew the closer they got to the rock plateau. The guardian dogs were alerted by the approaching visitors a while back. They were excited; they had not had any physical visitors for at least a Jupiter cycle. Their flesh could be smelt from halfway across the river. The stench of the human, the mouldy whiff of a hobgoblin, and ... was that a cat they could detect? They could not be sure, if not a cat, then some other tasty creature was coming a calling.

'Call my name and I will return you to the world of mathematical law,' growled Charon, as the passengers disembarked the ferry. The heat from the fires embraced their bodies as they advanced forward, towards the opening to the Underworld and its two guardians: fierce-looking, sleek, black sharp-toothed dogs. Where was the third guardian?

'Greetings, travellers. My name is Religion,' welcomed one of the dogs, 'and this is my brother, Politics,' pointing his nose towards the other. 'And Media is sleeping off his hangover,' he continued.

'Is that a cat I smell?' interjected Politics, smelling Lucifer, but not seeing him hiding behind Rufus and Percival. He was sure it was a cat.

'I wish to speak with the Goddess Eoaster,' commanded Rufus, like a King would to his hunting dogs; it was the only way he knew how to talk to dogs. They respected leadership, thought Rufus, but these, as it was, responded badly to authority. The pair of dogs began snarling at Rufus, threatening to launch an attack on him. Percival stepped forward, taking the attention of the dogs onto him.

'Friends, we come in peace,' copying a line he had heard used often by Rufus. 'We only wish to enter into the Underworld for a short time, fetch a goddess, and return.'

'Fetch a Goddess?' queried Religion, losing interest in the human and staring questioningly at the hobgoblin. 'What do you mean, "fetch a Goddess"?' Meanwhile, Politics had discovered a new plaything. When Percival moved forward it exposed Lucifer to the dog. There was a cat. Politics strode towards the travellers with cat essence drowning his senses, causing Religion to stop his questioning of the hobgoblin and question Politics instead.

'What are you doing Politics?' he barked.

'I'm hunting cat,' Politics replied, closing quickly on the trio. Suddenly, a terrifying banshee scream echoed around the cavern, putting the shivers up even Religion and Politics and stopping them in their tracks for a brief moment. It certainly did not help the nerves of Rufus and Percival. Lucifer looked up at Rufus and Percival and shouted,

'Run,' before releasing another death-defying scream. He raced off at speed across the plateau, towards the cavern wall; a dead end as far as Rufus and Percival could see. Politics gave chase at once; he loved a bit of sport before the kill. Religion followed the chase, instinctively leaping after Politics.

'Run,' Percival shouted to Rufus, whose mind was still with the hunt. 'Run,' Percival shouted again, this time giving Rufus a shove in the direction of the cave entrance: the empty, unguarded entrance to the Underworld. 'Run! Lucifer can look after himself, just run.'

When they reached the entrance they carried on running, aware that a third dog, Media, was sleeping off a hangover somewhere. They would just have to hope that Lucifer escaped the dogs and worry about getting out when the time came. Rufus's senses were awakened by the vibration of the growl, half a heartbeat before the sound arrived. Then the full blast of the hatred that came with the growl punched into both Rufus and Percival as they turned to face Media. Media was twice the size of Religion and Politics, but much of that size was fat. Media's belly wobbled beneath him as he barked.

'The cat is dead,' Media hissed, 'and soon you two will be as well.'

'Wait,' shouted Percival, pulling something from the pocket of his cloak: fresh strips of young lamb. He threw one towards Media, it landed tantalizingly at the dog's feet.

'You can't bribe me,' snarled Media, as Percival threw another strip of meat at him, then another.

Media looked at the meat. It was fresh meat, much better than the rubbish he got fed by Cruachan. The smell seeped into his juice buds.

'I will eat this before I enjoy eating you both in a moment,' Media smirked. He took the three strips of lamb in one mouthful, then sat blocking the way, chewing on the meat. Rufus went for Fireblade, but the dagger was out of reach in the Otherworld. 'You fool; you thought you could use your magic dagger in the Underworld. The Middle world, your world of matter, separates the Otherworld from this world. You would have been better leaving it in the coney warren,' growled Media. Percival threw the last two strips of meat to the Hellhound who gratefully lapped them up. 'News travels fast between the two worlds. The messengers have been busy these last few days,' Media divulged, swallowing the last of the meat and licking his teeth in anticipation of ripping the man and the hobgoblin to bits. Suddenly his world began to spin and jump, and his breathing became laboured. Media dropped to the floor as a soft glaze filled his eyes and his energy levels evaporated in an instant. His body was present, but no one was at home.

Rufus looked at Percival in amazement, 'That was clever planning,' heralded Rufus, 'Well done.'

'It was Lizzy's idea,' Percival admitted, 'she prepared a sacrificial lamb, for the cause. I should add that her and Drui'en concocted the potion in the meat that has sent Media to the Forest of Rainbows for a time. It was meant for all three of them. I don't know how long we have but we had better hurry before it wears off.' They marched off triumphantly, to the end of the short tunnel, where a large expanse of a city was carved in the depths of the earth. They were in the Underworld; Lucifer was missing in action, but Rufus and Percival were in.

EOASTER GREETINGS

Rufus and Percival found themselves standing before a large city carved into a mountain of rock, with buildings and streets and parks and trees. Ghostly shadowy people drifted through bustling thoroughfares.

'Look, there are animals here too,' noticed Percival, pointing towards the outskirts of the underworld city. The city spiralled its way up the mountain, culminating at the very top, in a white stone palace of sorts, with a deep red roof. Above the mountain was, what looked to Rufus, a sky. A blue sky, with wispy clouds and a very orange sun that painted the world in his essence, much like you would get at sunrise and sunset above ground. A strong wooden bridge offered the way across a deep ravine to the city and without further thought, Rufus and Percival crossed. The first thing they noticed was that the spirit inhabitants took little notice of them wandering the streets, only really acknowledging them when they stopped to discuss a plan of sorts.

'We could be looking for Eoaster forever, just wandering aimlessly like this,' confided Rufus, who had not had a plan figured out for when he arrived here. He was hoping something would fall into place. As he looked around the city, it seemed to him that they needed to get to higher ground to at least get an idea of the place. Small lanes led upwards towards the temple, which were less crowded, with fewer wandering spirits, and, more direct.

'Up there,' Rufus pointed to a narrow path leading upwards. During their short rest they noticed a crowd had started to gather around them, discussing them with each other but only silence came out of their mouths. When they moved, the spirits' gazes remained focused on where they had stood for several heartbeats, before forgetting what the fuss was all about and drifting away to continue their existence.

'If only we could ask somebody,' declared Percival. 'It would make things much easier,' he uttered under his breath, following Rufus up a steep path that led to the spiral street higher up the mountain with a better view of the landscape.

It was on this higher level, when Rufus was getting some idea of the lay-out, the order of the place, that he saw her: his Queen, Carolyn. His wife had caught his gaze as he was surveying the second level, which was less busy than the first. It seemed more orderly in some way, with the buildings less shambolic and less spirits drifting around. But one of those spirits belonged to his dead Queen; his beloved Carolyn, daughter of the Great Dalan of Gymry and the mother of his missing son, Uriens. Perhaps she knew where Uriens was now; he'd been taken from Rufus so soon after the

Queen's death. God, how he had missed her. It would be coming up three cycles, come the autumn equinox, since she was taken by the Lord of Death. She caught an infection giving birth to Uriens and died days later. For a while, Rufus had his son to remind him of her, easing the pain in his heart a little. Then, at Samhain, he was stolen in the night, when the veil between the three worlds were at their thinnest. He had to talk to her. Rufus began to walk towards Carolyn's spirit, who at that moment saw him walking towards her and cried a tear of joy.

'No Rufus,' shouted Percival, the instant he saw Rufus stride towards the motionless ghost. As Rufus began to formulate words in his mind to say to Carolyn, a sharp pain around his skull registered for a moment before bright stars invaded his vision. They were replaced by a darkness that was both to be feared and to seek solace in.

When Rufus came round, Percival was leaning over him, calling out his name. Rufus felt woozy trying to figure out what had happened, one moment Carolyn, the next, darkness.

'You ok, Rufus?' Percival was asking. 'I'm sorry I had to hit you, but you were going to speak to one of the spirits. I had to do something.' Rufus was lucky and he knew it. If Percival had not intervened, Rufus would be spending the rest of time here, in the world of souls, drifting through the realm in search of a purpose in death. Rufus's senses recovered sufficiently for him to stand with the help of Percival pulling him up.

'You did the right thing there, my friend; thanks,' breathed a grateful Rufus. 'What did you hit me with?'

'My head,' replied Percival, 'I have a very hard skull,' he beamed proudly. Rufus spotted another short cut up the mountain, another lane that led uphill between some high stone walls. Rufus took one last look around at the ghosts as they breezed by, hoping to see her for one last time. He pulled himself together, gave Percival a good slap on the back and continued to the next level up the mountain.

Two pillars supporting a capstone faced Rufus and Percival at the top of the lane. Carved into the capstone was the word NETZACH.

'What does Netzach mean?' Percival asked.

'I have not a clue,' answered Rufus. 'I think it is Hebrew,' he guessed, taking a long look down the lane before stepping over the threshold between the pillars. 'I do not think it is anything to worry about,' confided Rufus as they entered the next kingdom. An entirely different scene from the last two levels greeted them. Gone were the rows of buildings and crowds of ghosts. Rufus and Percival found themselves in a countryside landscape bathed in a yellow light. A twisting path ran alongside the mountain, towards a circle of stones on top of a hill. To the left of the path, open fields led to the mountain edge. What Rufus could only describe as the "Garden of Eden" dominated the right of the path.

'Beautiful,' whispered Rufus. In the distance they could see two ghosts slowly breezing down the hill towards them.

'Remember Rufus, no speaking to them,' Percival warned. Rufus smiled, rubbing his head; he was finished trying to talk to the dead. Despite being surrounded by nature, an eerie silence deafened them. There was no breeze to rustle the leaves, no animals or birds singing in the garden. In fact, there was nothing going on at all, except the two ghosts closing in on them as they walked up the hill. The ghosts were a man and a woman who ignored Rufus and Percival as they swept past them, continuing their journey down the path.

Around the next corner, a donkey-headed man holding a staff stood at the edge of the field. He was dressed in a white tunic that had planetary symbols etched onto it. Rufus and Percival stopped in their tracks when they saw him. The donkey-headed man pointed his staff at the pair announcing,

'I am Elous, the Lord of Magic. What is your purpose here in the house of Victory?'

'Don't answer him, Rufus,' Percival pleaded when Rufus took a step forward towards the creature.

'I do not think he is one of the dead,' Rufus whispered back to Percival, 'he is a solid creature, not like the wisps of smoke of the ghosts.' Percival felt unsure and gave Rufus a look to say so.

'You think I am one of the dead?' roared donkey-head. 'If I have never lived, then I can never die,' he retorted to Percival. 'It is rare to get visitors coming from the world of time to this world. I can only assume you are lost, or you are a pair of thieves looking to steal a magic object from the Underworld.'

'We are not thieves, my friend,' explained Rufus, 'We are on a mission to find the Goddess Eoaster and ask for her to help a young child who is in trouble with a powerful druid.'

'The Goddess is not in this realm,' replied Elous, lowering his staff.

'Perhaps the Witch of Endor knows of her whereabouts. She is the Guardian of the Threshold and prepares the Way for the seeker. She is the reconciler of Light and Dark,' donkey-head offered.

'Do you know where we can find this Witch of Endor?' pleaded Rufus.

'The witch you seek dwells in the Secret Valley.' Elous replied. 'It is up to you to find the Secret Valley yourself,' he concluded, waving the pair onwards.

'I don't suppose the valley is signposted?' Percival countered, before following Rufus up the hill.

There was not much chance of the Secret Valley to the left of the path in the open fields towards the edge of the mountain, so Rufus and Percival concentrated their efforts to the right, looking for clues in the bushes and trees that flourished up the mountainside.

'Here's a path,' called Percival, revealing a narrow, overgrown path through the garden that veered to the right and out of sight after around fifty paces. Rufus looked up the path, bordered on both sides by waist-high hedges and shadowed in places by trees.

'I do not think so Percival,' Rufus enthused, after some thought. 'It is not a valley,' he deduced. 'And it certainly is not secret. No, this is not the right path.' Rufus concluded and continued up the hill.

The path veered to the left of the hill with the stone circle on top, which led into a valley, towards a dolmen on the opposing bank. Not very secret though, thought Rufus.

'Look here,' called Percival, pulling back the branches of a bush to expose a dark path up a small valley. Rufus walked back to his friend; he had missed it completely.

'Looks promising,' he told Percival and shoved his way past the branches onto the path. He and Percival followed the winding track up through the valley, the sharp thorns tearing at his cloak and making it hard going. Suddenly, they were faced with an old woman, dressed in black, barring their way. The Witch of Endor, thought Rufus.

'Turn back from the Secret Valley,' the old woman shrieked. 'Thou canst pass this way,' she continued, producing a ball of white energy between her hands. 'Unless you both wish to be turned into frogs,' the witch threatened.

Rufus looked hard at the witch. He did not want to become a frog, but he could not give up either.

'I seek the audience of the Goddess Eoaster, dear witch; do you know where she can be found?' Rufus requested firmly.

The witch replied,

'To the foolish gaze the created world is terror, the terror of darkness. The Goddess dwells in the Light. Now return, for thou canst pass this way.'

'The Goddess is required in the world of mortality, of time and change. A young girl's life is at stake. Please let us pass.' Rufus pleaded.

'Thine eyes canst bear the dazzling radiance of the path ahead; return now or prepare to spend the rest of eternity as frogs,' the witch responded coldly.

Rufus tried one more time,

'I must help the young girl; she is being abused by a powerful druid and only Eoaster can stop him. Please let me pass.'

It seemed a reasonable request, thought the witch, who hated injustices, especially the manipulation of the powerful over the innocent ones. 'Tell me my name and I will allow you, brave warrior, to pass but the hobgoblin stays here,' she demanded. 'I sit at the left-hand side of creation, as the feminine power of the universe, whereas Metatron sits at the right-hand side and is the masculine power.'

Rufus thought about the question. The answer lay hidden somewhere in the shadows of his memory. Who was Metatron's consort? Rufus thought back to his New Sarum training, where divine beings were studied alongside astrology and weapon training. Metatron was the angel of the presence divine, and his consort was the angel ... Sandy ... Sandal ... Sandalphon. His consort was Sandalphon!

'Your name is Sandalphon,' declared Rufus. 'The Angel Sandalphon.'

The witch lowered her arms, allowing the ball of energy to dissipate, and ushered Rufus past. Rufus thanked her and gave a small wave to Percival, who had found a small rock to sit on while the King continued his quest up the valley.

Soon he found himself at a cave entrance that went into the side of the mountain. The word TIPHARETH was carved above the entrance. A short tunnel led to an expanse of green countryside that had no boundaries as far as Rufus could see. There was no path to follow, just rolling hills and valleys. In the sky, a large eye looked at him without judgement, just observing the stranger who had entered into the world of beauty. The eye made Rufus nervous, watching him as he rambled up one of the hills in search of the Goddess. He hoped for a better view of the realm from the top of the hill and to get a better idea of where to start looking for Eoaster. At the top, Rufus called out to the Goddess, hoping to attract her attention. He did attract the attention of a dove that swooped down to greet him. Rufus looked at the dove as it landed at his feet and began pecking at the ground.

'I am looking for Eoaster,' Rufus said, as the dove looked up for a moment, before continuing to peck at the ground, ignoring the King's request. Rufus tried again, 'Please can you help me in my search for the Goddess, pretty dove? I need her help.' The dove carried on pecking at the ground until she had picked up a tiny blue plant with her beak. She took off, dropping it into the hand of Rufus and telling him to "eat" before flying off into the distance. Rufus put the plant into his mouth, chewed, swallowed, and waited.

'I am Eoaster,' a voice boomed from behind Rufus. He turned to face a beautiful dark-haired woman dressed in a green flowing dress. 'I am Eoaster,' the vision repeated. 'Who seeks my time?' she challenged Rufus.

'Greetings Eoaster,' Rufus replied, 'I am King Rufus of Vindocladia, and I need your help to save a young girl from a powerful druid.'

'I do not meddle in the affairs of man or druid anymore,' the Goddess replied. 'Now go; you have wasted your time here.' she concluded and prepared to leave.

'No, wait,' pleaded Rufus. 'A young girl is being abused by a powerful druid on the Isle of the Dead and I am informed that only you can stop it.'

Eoaster pondered his last comment. She did not like what she was hearing.

'Continue,' Eoaster requested, turning back towards Rufus. Rufus explained the best he could all the events that had led him to ask for her help.

'Soon the news will be out, and the people of Portland will try and lynch Balise, who will use his power to repel them. People will die, the island will be split, and a young girl's torment will continue,' asserted Rufus. 'If you decide to do nothing,' threatened Rufus, 'I will confront the druid myself. Whatever the outcome, I swear I will!'

'Give me a moment,' Eoaster asked, and disappeared in a flash, which took Rufus by surprise making him dizzy and needing to sit down. It felt as if he had been in the Underworld for half of his life. A cold chill rushed down his spine making him shiver. He wondered if it was all real, or if he was still lying unconscious in the witch's house, yet to wake from his dice with death in the quarry. He felt tired, drained of all his energy. Rufus wondered how Percival was getting on, waiting with the Witch of Endor and then his mind drifted to Lucifer and the chasing hounds. Was the cat still alive? Rufus and Percival still had to get past the dogs on their way out.

Rufus was aware of a flash of light behind him; Eoaster had returned. The King regained enough of his strength to stand and face her.

'Will you help?' he asked.

Eoaster put her hands on her hips before replying.

'King Rufus of Vindocladia, I accept your request. Druid Balise is a cancer in the community and must answer for his actions. I will gladly rid your world of this foul creature.' She paused for a heartbeat before continuing, staring Rufus full in the eyes, 'I cannot come right away; I will have to arrange things to get out of this world. I cannot just up and walk away. I have to phase my energy to be able to comply with your world, which takes time, before I can pay a visit to Balise. But it will be before the next moonrise in your world, I promise.'

'Thank you,' beamed Rufus, ecstatic he had succeeded in his mission, but also apprehensive that he still needed to get out alive.

'Ask Sandalphon to give you a potion to perk you up on your way out. Ask her for an Eoaster Egg - she will know what you mean,' instructed the Goddess, smoothing her dress out around her stomach. She gave Rufus a beaming smile before turning into a flash of light and disappearing into another dimension. Rufus felt his strength and courage rise with every step he took back towards the gateway he had entered this world by.

Rufus was soon through the tunnel and making his way down the Secret Valley towards his friend and the witch. He found them in deep discussion.

'You are not separate from the life you experience; you are the life that is experienced,' the witch was explaining to Percival when Rufus appeared. Percival leapt off his rock and lurched over to hug the King. Rufus hugged the hobgoblin back; it really was great to see the little fellow.

'You were only gone a heartbeat,' said Percival as the pair separated. 'Did you find Eoaster in that time?' he asked.

'I was gone for more than a heartbeat my young friend,' replied Rufus, 'she was not easy to find; but she will take on Balise before moonrise.' Rufus turned to the witch, 'Eoaster tells me I have to try one of your excellent Eoaster Eggs.' The witch smiled before answering,

'It will take a short time to concoct the potion, but it will fill you both up with strength and courage for your journey out.'

DEAD CATS DON'T MEOW

Refreshed, Rufus and Percival thanked the Witch of Endor for her kindness and left her to make their way down the Secret Valley and with luck, out of the Underworld alive. Percival questioned Rufus about his experience with the Goddess, but the King did not want to talk about it. Not that it was a bad experience, it had just exhausted him, and he wanted to keep his mind focused on the journey out. It did not take long for them to reach the entrance to the Secret Valley and get back on to the path that led down the mountain. The same two ghostly figures that had passed them on their way up the hill were now gliding up the path towards them and as before the spirits ignored the odd pair. Elous the donkey- faced guardian bid them a safe exit as they went past him.

'Everyone seems friendly here,' stated Percival, enjoying his adventure in the realm of the dead.

'We still have a long way to go. This is the least of it.' Rufus reminded the hobgoblin, 'We still have to deal with the dogs guarding the entrance.' he continued. Both of their thoughts turned to Lucifer and hoped in the name of the Goddess that he was still alive.

Soon they were at the threshold between TIPHERETH and the lower world of HOD, where Rufus had encountered his dead wife. He wanted to see her again but at the same time it would be better if he did not. He had so much to ask her, but if he uttered one word to her he would have to remain in the Underworld forever. No, it was better for them not to come across Carolyn on the way out. With their eyes focused on the ground in front of them, the pair hurried down the slope as quickly as they could without taking any notice of the world about them. Rufus spotted the entrance to the lane out of HOD ahead of him, between the stone buildings, and quickened his pace, with Percival close behind. Ten paces away from the exit with his heart pounding, a relief began to ease the anxiety that Rufus felt, when suddenly she was there, standing between him and the alleyway. His heart stopped.

'Don't say anything Rufus,' Percival called out when he saw the woman. Rufus felt enchanted; his body was motionless, and his mind was totally focused on the vision before him. Luckily for Rufus, his tongue was frozen in time too.

It was Carolyn who spoke,

'Rufus, my love. You look awful; you have not shaven in a while. And when was the last time you washed?'

Rufus wanted to speak to his Queen, but he was still struck dumb. And anyway, Rufus knew that Percival was watching his back and would not hesitate to headbutt him unconscious again if he had to.

Carolyn continued,

'I miss you, dearest. I love you still. Even in death, my heart pounds with your memory.'

'Don't say anything Rufus,' Percival reminded the King.

Carolyn smiled at the hobgoblin,

'Do not worry, my green friend, brave hobgoblin. His mouth is silenced so he cannot speak, even if he wanted to.' Facing Rufus again Carolyn continued, 'Darling husband, I feel your pain; your heart is scarred. I am well here, slowly making my way up the mountain, to KETHER and rebirth. One day we will be reunited.' Rufus's heart thumped at the thought and memories of their short life together came flooding into his mind. Then he thought of his missing baby son Uriens, and sadness overcame his heart.

'Our son is well,' Carolyn continued, seeing the sadness seep from her husband's heart. 'He is being held captive in The Valley of No Return, in the Enchanted Forest of Broceliande across the channel. Morgan Le Fey has him.'

Suddenly a frown grew on Carolyn's face as she reached into Rufus's soul. 'You have loved another woman,' she cried out, in despair at her husband. 'Barely three cycles have I gone, and I see you have placed my memory in a dark forest so you could lay with someone else. How could you?'

Rufus tried to think what she was on about.

'Of course, Morr'igan the evening before,' he thought. 'That was not love; that was only pleasure. It was an action in the heat of the moment, a bewitching time as the sun sank beneath the horizon.'

'But did you think of me?' cried Carolyn. 'I may be dead, but I am still your Queen.' A silence ensued while Carolyn decided how to respond next.

'Let's go now Rufus,' Percival shouted to his friend, at the same time as he stood between the ghost and Rufus. He stared into the eyes of the man, grabbing hold of his arms. 'Let's go now Rufus or I will have to headbutt you again.' Rufus was still frozen to the spot and his voice still silent, but he knew he had to get away. He tried to say sorry to his wife, but his tongue was still not working.

'I will let you go, my King, for I still love you. I thought you still loved me, but I guess not. But before you go, I should warn you Morr'igan is not to be trusted. Did you not learn anything from Morgan Le Fey? Even their names are similar. What do you know about this woman? Nothing!'

Movement returned to Rufus's body, and he nodded towards Percival, to let him know he was in control of his functions again. He looked past his friend, towards the face of his unhappy, betrayed wife. Guilt invaded his heart as he gave Carolyn a weak smile, before following Percival down the lane.

Shortly they were rushing down the shambolic streets of YESOD amid the crumbling buildings, towards the bridge back over the abyss. Rufus wished he had brought a skin of water with him, but it was forbidden; only eat and drink what is offered to you in the Underworld, Pellinore had cautioned. He stopped at the bridge and had one last look at the Underworld city that reached high into the cavern.

'I am glad that is over Percival,' Rufus declared, getting his composure and strength back. 'But we still have to get past the hounds yet. You have any ideas, my friend?' he asked, totally out of ideas himself.

'I have a crystal that will enchant the stupid fat dog, but it will only work on one dog at a time.' Percival boasted. 'The Witch of Endor gave it to me while you were visiting the Goddess.' A smile crept over Rufus's lips; he had not expected the hobgoblin to have an answer. He was not expecting his friend to ask him a question just then, either. 'Who is Morr'igan?' Percival beamed, hands on hips, waiting for an answer.

'What?' Rufus responded, a little bemused.

'Who is Morr'igan?' Percival repeated. 'I heard that ghost talking to you about her.'

Who was Morr'igan? thought Rufus. He had only just met her. He really did not know anything about her, only she was a witch; a beautiful witch at that, mind you. And she possibly had a connection to his son's disappearance.

'Now is not the right time, Percival.' Rufus responded. 'I will tell you all about her when we get back to our world.' Without looking over into the abyss under the bridge, Rufus and Percival strode boldly to the other side to face the dogs.

Media sat defiantly, blocking the tunnel with his vast bulk. He seemed larger, somehow, than before.

'I've been waiting for you two.' The dog growled. 'I am hungry, and I am angry, and I am going to eat you right now.' Percival whipped out the piece of crystal that the witch had given him and pointed it towards Media. Percival closed his eyes to concentrate on what the witch had told him,

'With the power of Sandalphon I command you to be a tiny spider. So be it!' Media glared at the hobgoblin for a short time before letting out a great roar. He tensed his muscles in his rear legs, ready to pounce on his prey, when suddenly a vibration thumped into his body, causing him to let out a muffled whine. When his senses returned, Media was ready to hurl himself at the prey again, when he saw the man and the hobgoblin had transformed into giants. 'You are a tiny spider and if you don't run away, I will stamp on you,' informed Percival, waving the pink crystal in front of him. Media did not have a clue what was going on. It was the second time these visitors to Cruachan's Cave had tricked him somehow. He had no other option but to retreat and run away to hide down a passage in the tunnel.

'Can't you use that trick on the other dogs?' Rufus remarked, as they continued along the tunnel.

'Not while the big dog thinks he is a spider. I will have to release him before I can enchant another dog, and then there will still be the third dog to deal with.'

Soon they were back at the cave entrance and at the fiery plateau that separated them from the river and their return to the outer world. They feared the worst for Lucifer and were looking about for Politics and Religion ready to confront them, but no animal stirred anywhere that they could see. Then the piercing call of a meow floated into their consciousness, not a distressed meow of a cat in agony, but a calm and collected meow of a cat that is content. Lucifer was alive!

Rufus and Percival strode out of the cave to see that at the edge of the cave wall, Lucifer was sat on a rock between Politics and Religion. They seemed to be arguing amongst themselves, totally unaware of the man and hobgoblin looking on.

'What is going on?' called Percival, 'We thought you were dead.'

'Dead cats don't meow,' Lucifer responded with a large grin on his face. 'I got talking to the dogs about how Media was using them, making them do all the work while he stuffed himself on the riches that came with guarding the Underworld. I told them Media was nothing but propaganda, using Politics and Religion to create fear in anyone they should come into contact with.'

'I am impressed,' enthused Rufus, as Politics turned to look at him before returning his focus on what rubbish Religion was going on about. The two dogs were so engrossed with each other they did not notice the cat join the man and the hobgoblin making their way to the river.

'You weren't gone long,' purred Lucifer, as they reached the river. 'I guess you did not get into the Underworld?' the cat continued.

'We were gone for half a day at least,' retorted Percival. 'We got a message to the Goddess, and she is going to give Balise his comeuppance before the sun sets.'

'Well, for me, you have only been gone a few heartbeats; not long enough to do all that you say you did,' argued Lucifer. 'The time must travel much slower in the Underworld,' decided Rufus. 'We were certainly in the Underworld for a considerable time,' he concluded, before summoning up the ferryman. 'Charon, I call on you to return us across the river back to the world of matter and time.'

After a short time, a horn blasted from upriver, and a cool mist floated with the sound down past the three adventurers. From that mist came the ferryman, who halted his boat next to Rufus and his comrades.

'To which world do you require?' Charon growled.

'Our world,' called Percival.

'The world of day and night,' added Lucifer.

'The world of space and time,' concluded Rufus.

'There are many such worlds,' declared the ferryman. 'From what is your world created?' he questioned. The three travellers thought about the question. From what was their world created? None of them knew.

'It was created by the spirits?' Rufus guessed, wrongly. Charon pulled a timepiece from his filthy, ragged cloak as if to say time was running out. They had no clue what their world was created from. Then Lucifer remembered what the ferryman had said to them when they first encountered him: "Call my name and I will return you to the world of mathematical law." Lucifer did not understand what it meant but it had to be the answer. The cat looked defiantly at the ferryman, announcing,

'We wish to return to the world of mathematical law.' Charon put his timepiece away and ushered the trio on board. Rufus and Percival looked at Lucifer in astonishment. Neither of them had expected the cat to be so clever.

'Well done, my feline friend,' beamed Rufus, as they clambered onto the ferry. Lucifer beamed from ear to ear. He could not wait to boast of his heroism to his friends.

Soon they were on the other side of the river, the side of the living and breathing. All three were relieved and felt the stress evaporate from their bodies. They only had the short walk of the dark tunnel to do before returning to the outside. The cool breeze felt welcome as the light at the end of the tunnel appeared before them. They could hear the chanting of Pellinore still calling on the moon.

How long had they been inside the cave? Surely not a whole day had gone by?

Then they emerged into the day, very much as they had left it, with the moon just disappearing below the horizon and the old wizard still chanting to the heavens. At the sight of the three explorers, Pellinore stopped his mantra and welcomed the trio back into the world of the living. They had made it.

'How long have we been gone?' enquired Rufus, still a little confused with the time side of things. Pellinore laughed at the question before replying,

'There is no time inside of Cruachan's Cave. You have only been gone from this world for several heartbeats; no more than that.' Rufus scratched his head and decided not to question the strange phenomena; he was just relieved that they had successfully completed their mission. The Goddess Eoaster had been summoned to rid Portland of the evil Balise and save Bridget's daughter Drui'en from his grasp. He was pleased with himself. The early morning air smelt good. Rufus thanked his friends, patting Percival on the back and giving Lucifer a head scratch, leaving the cat purring in pleasure.

Pellinore returned to his cave in the side of the cliff, while the three heroes made their way to the Infirmary gates to meet up with Lizzy Penn and the gatekeeper. In the distance they saw that Lizzy and the gatekeeper had guests: several druids waited with them, obviously wanting to congratulate the three on their daring exploits. They were in for a shock when one of the druids called out for the three to be arrested.

'Take the man to the Archdruidess,' the leader of the druids announced, as two druids came forward to grab hold of Rufus. The King was too stunned to struggle.

'Take the hobgoblin to the prison,' the leader ordered, 'And have the cat taken to ... Where is the cat?'

Everyone looked around for Lucifer, but he had crept away in the long grass.

'Dead cats don't meow,' informed Percival, as he and Rufus were led away from the Infirmary.

'Why are we under arrest?' Rufus demanded, his mind beginning to clear and his normal senses returning. 'We have done nothing wrong,' he added, trying to shake himself free. 'What does the Archdruidess want from me?' he questioned, as his handlers tightened their grip on him.

'She wants your balls,' snarled the druid in charge. Just then, the sun emerged from behind the fort above the goddess temple and bathed the island in sunshine.

ALL THE KING'S MEN

It was a hot morning. The druids and their prisoners stopped off at the Goddess Temple overlooking the cove for a drink from the spring that flowed from the cliff face. Rufus took the water in his hands and wetted his head. It had been a long day already, despite the sun only recently hovering over the eastern horizon.

'What is this all about?' Rufus quizzed one of his captors. The tall druid merely shrugged his shoulders and mumbled something about invaders arriving. 'Invaders?' queried Rufus, 'What invaders?' Before his question could be answered another druid spoke.

'Thanks to you, Lord Belvedore's farm has been raided and hundreds of conies released back into the wild.'

'Is this why the Archdruidess wants to see me?' questioned Rufus, still unsure of why he had been arrested.

'No,' the druid replied, taking a scooped handful of cold water for himself. 'There has been a much more serious incident that requires your explanation,' the druid continued. 'I cannot enlighten you any more than that. It is not my job to do so. But I would like you to know that we are grateful for your information concerning Lord Belvedore.

Unfortunately, he is still on the mainland and therefore still free.' Another druid with a long grey beard urged the group to get a move on,

'The Archdruidess is waiting for us; let's move.' With that, the group carried on the trek to the top of the island, to the hillfort. Rufus and Percival walked in silence, both reflecting on their experiences in the Underworld.

When they reached the hillfort, Percival was led away somewhere, while four druids escorted Rufus to the large, round house at the centre of the fort. It was the residence of the Archdruidess. One of the druids went inside, leaving Rufus wondering what all the fuss was about. Soon he was ushered into the dark, cool, round building to meet the druid leader. When his eyes got used to the darkness inside, the King was aware of the foreboding presence of the Archdruidess. She had her back towards him, her long brown hair reaching to her waist. Then she turned towards him and waved his guards away with a flick of her hand, leaving the two of them alone. 'Please, take a seat,' the Archdruidess spoke in a neutral tone. Rufus was happy to sit down and take the weight off his feet. The Archdruidess passed him a cup of water, which Rufus gulped down in one. When he had finished and put the cup down on the table between them, the tone of the Archdruidess changed from neutral to anger.

'A spy has been captured during the night,' she barked at Rufus. 'He tells me that he works for King Rufus of Vindocladia, as the General of the King's men who, as we speak, are making their way across the pebble beach, armed to the teeth ready for battle.' Rufus was trying to make sense of what the woman was saying. Why on earth would his army be on their way to the island? Before he could make any sort of comment, the Archdruidess continued, 'We are ready for war,' she screamed, banging her fists on the table, causing an orange crystal to jump in the air. Rufus tried to calm the woman, insisting that if it was his army, they were not here to invade.

'I have no idea as to why my soldiers are here,' Rufus declared, 'But I can assure you they are not here to invade.' Rufus brushed his hair back while he tried to think of why his men were here. 'Perhaps something has happened at home, and they need to contact me. Let me see my General so I can sort this out,' Rufus offered.

The Archdruidess thought for a moment, then called in one of the guards waiting outside.

'Take the prisoner to see his General, to find out what is going on,' the Archdruidess ordered the guard. 'Get back to me as soon as you can; I need to put this to bed as quickly as possible.'

On the way to the prison, Rufus was aware of dark clouds floating in from the west, moving towards Portland. Rain was on the way. The King was led through the gates to one of the prison huts down the south wall. Inside was his General, Griff Richards, a loyal and brave warrior who had served under Rufus for half his life. Both were glad to see each other and hugged before being separated by the guards.

'What are you doing here?' questioned Rufus. The General told Rufus that he was not a spy, but he had become concerned when Lizzy Penn had informed them that the King had been put into prison on the island. He had decided to come and rescue him.

'We could not come over on the ferry with our weapons, so we marched to Abbotesbyrig and came along the pebbled beach to get you back.' Griff explained how the army had always tailed the King on all his adventures, ever since the death of his Queen. They were worried about him getting into trouble roaming the land on his own. Rufus was not sure whether to be angry or glad that his men had always tailed him on his journeys. He guessed he should be pleased that they cared so much about him to keep an eye on him.

The King's men had reached the outskirts of the small village of Chiswell and were facing a druid army waiting patiently with their staffs for the order from the Archdruidess to attack the invaders. The King's soldiers had taken up a defensive position behind the rocks on the beach, waiting for news back from General Griff Richards or for the druids to start the attack. Either way, the soldiers were very nervous of fighting the druids with their magic, which was a far superior weapon than the bronze swords and wooden spears they had. No matter, they were the soldiers of their King and would fight to the death for him if need be.

Back with the Archdruidess, Rufus had assured her that the army was just concerned about their King and was no threat to the island.

'Let me reassure my army,' Rufus proposed. 'When they see that I am well, they will be happy to leave the island and wait for me in Wick.' The Archdruidess agreed to this and ordered the release of the King's General.

'But you,' she reminded Rufus, 'still have your sentence to serve. After you have spoken to your soldiers, you must return to Bridget's house for the night until we decide what to do with you. Your men can camp at the base of the island tonight if they promise not to hunt the conies. We shall supply food and drink for them and in return they must promise to leave at first light tomorrow.'

Rufus was escorted down the hill to meet his men, joined by Griff a little while later. Three priestesses and several druids had arrived with around a dozen pigs and several bottles of mead for the troops. The men had gathered driftwood from the beach and heaped it into a pile for a fire just as the first drops of rain began to fall.

'Looks like a wet night,' declared Griff to the men.

'Aye, and not for the first time,' one of them replied, as they took care of the pigs and passed around the mead.

'I can't believe you are under house arrest,' complained Griff to his King. Rufus smiled; he would have liked to stay with his men, feasting and drinking, but he liked the idea of spending more time with the pretty witch. And at least he would be in the dry. Before he left, Rufus updated them on his adventure so far, as they sat around the spitting fire trying to cope with the blustery rain coming in off the sea. The cooks were preparing the pigs to roast over the fire, when a grey-bearded druid used some magic to place an invisible shield over the King's men to save them from the rain. Druids with stringed musical instruments that Rufus had never seen or heard before began to entertain the troops, while the priestesses made sure the mead was getting around to all the men. It was good, thought Rufus, that his men were having a good time after days of anxiety. They knew he was safe and would be joining them soon when he had finished his sentence in the quarry. His heart shuddered at the thought of working in the quarry again. As the sky began to darken, the grey-bearded druid reminded Rufus it was time to go.

'What has happened to my friend Percival?' Rufus asked, suddenly remembering his friend.

'The hobgoblin is well and is back at the Infirmary at the Beale, helping out the carers there. He has a talent for dealing with the inmates,' confirmed Greybeard. 'He has been asked to remain on the island and help the lost discover their minds.'

Rufus bid farewell to his men; the smell of roasting pork over the fire made him realise how hungry he was. The sun was close to setting and Rufus remembered Goddess Eoaster's promise that she would confront Balise before the fiery ball had set. He looked up towards the hillfort where Balise was but could see no evidence that he had been dispatched. Would the Goddess keep her promise? Rufus hoped she would; Bridget's daughter deserved a better life. If Eoaster had not carried out her promise by the morning, Rufus himself would deal with the druid. Fireblade was still at his disposal hidden in the Otherworld, but would it be a match for the magic of the druid? Rufus would worry about it in the morning. He was tired, hungry, and now wet through. He was looking forward to getting to Bridget's house to rest and hopefully eat.

He was not disappointed when he reached the home of the witch. A fire glowed at the centre of the room and the aroma of roasted pork invaded his senses. Rufus could feel his mouth water. 'The fire is calming to the soul,' Bridget informed him as Greybeard led Rufus into the building. Bridget ordered Rufus to get out of his wet clothes and into dry ones from her husband's wardrobe. Meanwhile, she and Greybeard discussed her plans.

The Druid Balise lit several candles in his hut as darkness began to bathe the island. He was busy, putting together a spell that would give him total power over the people of Portland. First, he had to get rid of the Archdruidess and her merciful ideals that were holding the might of druidry back. It was not their purpose to care for the weak and poor, but to control and rule the community for their own benefit. With their knowledge and magic, druids should be conquering and dominating new communities. Suddenly, a cold mist entered the hut carried by a cool breeze, causing the candles to flicker, and sending shadows skirting around the place. Balise was aware of a presence in the room and grabbed his wand, which was always at hand.

'Who is there?' the druid called out, creating a protection sphere around himself as he stood. He watched the mist expand and form into a person in front of him, slowly becoming the solid form of a woman clothed in a dress made from the mist that she had appeared from.

'Who are you? What do you want?' demanded Balise, raising his wand in preparation to dispel the spirit before him.

'I am the Goddess Eoaster,' the spirit answered, 'I am going to make you pay for your crimes against the children of this isle.'

Balise released an energy bolt from his wand that would surely send the ghost back to the Underworld. The hut lit up, blinding him momentarily, but he felt reassured when his vision returned, and he saw that the ghostly woman had disappeared. No female was a match for him—not even a goddess could harm him. He had learnt his arts from the Master himself, the fallen god called Satan. The Dark Lord had moved Balise up the ranks to be second-in-command of the small island community. Only the Archdruidess was above him and he had influenced enough of the brothers to see her as holding the Order back from its potential: to be masters of the universe. As Balise began to grin to himself, he became aware of an icy grip on the back of his neck; Eoaster still remained in his world. He turned quickly, raising his wand to attack the goddess, but suddenly found himself rising into the air, his balance and confidence ebbing away into the shadows lurking in his hut.

'You will pay for your diabolical deeds, Balise, this very evening,' Eoaster declared to the druid. 'Your time of abusing your power is over!' Balise waved his wand frantically at the goddess, screaming spells at her and cursing her, as he floated to the roof. Dark demons thundered into the hut and tore away his clothes, leaving him naked and exposed with his back glued to the roof. Eoaster took one of the candles, still flickering madly in the energy-imbued room, and held it under the groin of the druid. Balise cried out as the heat began to embrace his genitals.

'Please stop; what are you going to do? I was possessed by evil and had no control over what I was doing.' Eoaster removed the candle and replaced it on the table.

'I will not be the judge of your punishment, Balise,' the Goddess enlightened the druid. 'I will leave that task to the witch's daughter, Drui'en. She understands the wishes of all the children over the cycles whose lives you have invaded with your evil. It is she who will decide your fate.

GOOD VIBRATIONS

Rufus snuggled up to the fire at the centre of the room, dressed in warm, dry clothes. He accepted a drink from Bridget, who was sitting across from him on the other side of the fire.

'It is mead, made from the honey of bees,' Bridget informed him as he stared at the cup of orange liquid in his possession. 'I have added a few ingredients of my own to help us relax before retiring.' Bridget explained. Rufus sniffed at the drink before taking a sip. It warmed the cockles of his heart and left a fuzzy haze in his mind. It felt as if it was the first time he had actually relaxed since he first set off on this crazy adventure, not that he had been able to relax much before the quest. A blast of wind forced its way past the skin over the door, causing the smoke from the fire to envelop the witch, sending fingers of flame grasping towards the couple's thoughts as they drifted in the air. Bridget spluttered and moved around the fire to kneel next to Rufus and felt safe enough to put her head in his lap. Rufus put a comforting arm around her shoulders; he felt comfortable with the situation. He took another sip of mead, allowing the rich taste to linger on his tongue and allowing deep thoughts to form in his mind. He had always been aware of the magic found in the spirit world but had always been unable to reach the required discipline to visit and explore the world of the Gods and Goddesses, converse with the elementals and drink in the springs of wisdom. For whatever reason, like many others he was unable to penetrate the world of the astral, not for the want of trying. Suddenly Bridget awakened the King from his thoughts with a question of her own.

'What do you believe in? I mean what do you think living is all about? Why you are a King, and I am a witch?' Rufus gulped down the rest of his mead to give him time to think of a reply. It was not something he could answer in a brief sentence or two. 'I knew it was you watching the red goddess ceremony two nights ago.' Bridget continued, before Rufus had a chance to reply. 'I felt your gaze and accepted it into the circle to participate in the experience. Some of your energy is woven into the spell that we made that night. It is a good strong energy; if somewhat misguided.'

'What do you mean, misguided?' asked Rufus, slowly grasping the thought that some of his energy was a part of a spell. Dismissing the thought, Rufus was more concerned with the misguided bit.

'I am a King; I live in a castle surrounded by servants and subjects that serve at my command. I rule a thriving kingdom based on justice and order. What is misguided about that?'

'Then why are you unhappy?' replied Bridget. 'You feel you are lacking something important in your life. Your mind is surrounded by a material wealth devoid of anything spiritual. The world, the whole of the universe, is governed by the spiritual world, a world without any dross or thought. It's a world that will show you who you really are.'

Bridget removed herself from Rufus, refilling his cup with mead before pulling her chair over, sitting next to him and taking a long drink of her honey wine.

Another blast of wind found its way into the glowing room sending the flames into a merry dance. The mead was reaching into Rufus's mind, rearranging the furniture a little, dusting off the mantelpiece and opening the windows to the outside world. He breathed in the fresh air, exhaling it towards the fire, noticing moments later the reaction of a few of the flames when the breath reached the fire. How could such little effort affect such a powerful element as fire? mused Rufus.

'Everything is vibration,' Bridget announced, when she had made herself comfortable and poured herself another cup of mead. 'Everything is vibration, originating from the sound of the awakening Great Goddess while giving birth to the universe. The vibration became chaotic during the birth, becoming many different energies: some created physical manifestation, but the majority formed the spirit world. It is the home of the souls that are enmeshed in our bodies, yearning to visit there every now and again, to bathe in the radiance of the Goddess and the strength of the God. It is important to return home sometimes, if only to recharge our vigour for living.'

Rufus thought of his home—an age away in the East, cold, empty, and meaningless for a lot of the time. Here with the witch, he felt homely and more comfortable than he had felt anywhere that he could remember. He looked over towards Bridget, who was eyeing him back intently, her eyes radiating warmth that reached into Rufus's heart. He swilled the mead in his cup and had a good long sip before focusing back on what Bridget had said, imagining her as a vibrating mass of energy: her body, her words and even her thoughts. Rufus looked around the room, every part of it nothing more than a vibration, or, rather, millions of different vibrations working together to create a world that his senses could perceive. The room began to spin, and a sickness started to grow in his stomach. A warm bead of sweat trickled down his face. Rufus felt an arm rest across his back and Bridget's voice penetrating his mind; her calming words sounded poetic, almost musical.

'Drink this, it will calm your nerves and relax your mind a little,' Bridget told Rufus, as he sat up in his chair, taking hold the clay mug. 'Gulp it down in one,' Bridget added, 'It will clear your mind quicker and help you see more clearly.'

Rufus gulped the elixir down in one. It was very bitter after the sweetness of the mead. He became incredibly aware of where he was. Bridget had moved very close to him, leaving her arm over his shoulders, and resting her head against his. The pair of them glowed in the radiance of the fire like two planets coming together as they orbit the sun. A glow from their combined energies caused them both to experience a rise of vibrations inside their bodies. Bridget kissed Rufus on the top of his head before continuing her story.

'The energies formed themselves into two camps depending on the core of their makeup, either attracting or repelling other energy that they came across, creating the duality we have in the universe today: male and female, God and Goddess, Light and Dark.'

'So, you are saying,' interjected Rufus, 'that the gods and goddesses are only the different types of energy floating around in space?'

'And time,' added Bridget before continuing. 'Everything in the universe is the same thing; what sets everything apart is that each thing has a different frequency. The lower the vibration, the denser the energy is, creating the solid material world we see. The higher the vibration is, that's where a more spiritual world exists. The spirit world envelops the material world, and it is the events that occur in the spiritual world that play out in the material world.'

'So, we are only acting out the will of the gods,' Rufus responded, 'Then what you are saying is that we do not have control of our destinies,' Bridget thought for a second before answering,

'We communicate with the spirits by our deeds, with our thoughts even. The spirits can read us by what we do and think but unless we can listen to what they are trying to tell us, they will act out our desires as they see fit. That is not always what we really want.'

At that moment, another blast of wind rushed across the room, sending the flames into a frenzy once again and causing the shadows on the walls to join in the merry dance of the air. Rufus turned to look at Bridget and met her eyes staring back, calling for him to embrace her. He obliged, leaning over to her, bringing his mouth to touch hers. Their tongues explored each other, causing the vibrations of their bodies to rise another notch. Bridget moved off her chair on to Rufus's lap, their bodies beginning to shudder with the expectation of pleasure.

From out of the shadow, a loud clearing of a throat brought the lovers back to earth with a bump, glaring at the mass of black vibrating energy that stood before them.

'I didn't mean to make you jump,' grinned Lucifer, sauntering past them to his bed after an evening of telling of his heroic tale to the animals of the Grove. Rufus was too stunned to reply to the cat, as he made his way to the corner of the room and his cosiest chair. Bridget, who could not understand animal talk, moved back to her own chair at the presence of her cat, while Rufus wiped the embarrassment from his face.

'More mead, I think,' declared Bridget, blushing slightly, rising to fetch the calming mead.

Soon Lucifer was snoring in the corner of the room and Rufus and Bridget had again settled back in their chairs, enjoying the cosy atmosphere around the fire. Rufus was the first to interrupt the silence,

'Can you speak to the spirits?' Bridget folded her arms before replying,

'I communicate with the spirit world using symbols and mantras when the forces of the planets are favourable. I mean, it is easier to connect to the universe when the moon is full and is dominated by the motherly energy of the Red Goddess, especially if you need protection or want to heal. To have a glimpse of the future, it is best to request the services of the Crone energy of the Black Goddess of the waning moon, a time for reflection and contemplation. The White Goddess of the waxing moon radiates the maiden energy of creativity.'

'I did not realize the moon was so many things,' interrupted Rufus, as his concept of the moon changed. He had heard it referred to as a goddess before, but three Goddesses!

'She is much more than that,' stated Bridget, taking time out to take another sip of her drink. 'As well as her, you have the other planet energies to consider. The God and Goddess energies of Mercury, Venus, Mars, Jupiter, and Saturn—not forgetting the most important source of energy: the male energy of our star, the Sun.'

Bridget stopped talking to stoke the fire up a little, putting a seasoned log of ash into the cauldron. This caused the room to fill up with smoke until the log had reached the temperature of the fire and began to burn. Rufus watched as the smoke swirled away out of a vent in the top of the building.

'At the ceremony the other night, I saw the energies that you created: all different shapes and colours,' Rufus spoke, 'How did you do that?'

'First I did not create that energy. I only transferred it from one place to another, mixed it with other acquired energy, gave it a command, and sent it on to do the work. I did not create the energy, only the Gods and Goddesses can do that.' Bridget explained. 'I draw the energy down from the heavens and up from the earth to harness inside me, allowing it to mix with my inner energy, giving the force an objective. The blue spirit of the Goddess infuses with the green spirit of the earth and the white inner energy of myself into an electrifying, vibrating ball of purpose waiting for instructions.'

Rufus noticed his cup was empty and put it onto the floor. What Bridget was saying was mind boggling, but in a strange way it all made sense. A world that existed, which was not of this world but at the same time it was. The spirit world infused the world of matter and everything in it. 'It is the God that creates the material and the Goddess that shapes it.' Bridget continued. 'When the God and Goddess come together, a third force is created: the consciousness that gives the universe space, time, and all the life in it.

The Moon energy is a reflection of the Sun energy, so by using the energy of the Moon, the magic is already infused with the god, making it a powerful force to work with. Once harnessed inside the body and with the intent added, it is ready to be released into the sacred circle. It is already infused with the actions of the elementals, who are waiting to take the magic and its intent to its destination. In our case, it was to empower our crystals for a battle that will come from across the sea: the Bretagne's from Armorica.'

'How do you know that?' enquired Rufus, sitting up in his chair.

'From our prophetess, Fedel'ma,'

answered Bridget, 'She is blessed with being able to talk to the spirits. She prophesies at the Temple of Belisama, over-looking the cove.'

'I would like to speak to her, if that is possible,' announced Rufus, his thoughts turning towards his missing son—the original purpose of this jaunt to the Island of the Dead. 'I need to find my son.'

Bridget was silent for a time. It was the first time she had heard Rufus talk of his son, not that they had had much chance to talk since his recent arrival to Portland. She had not imagined him as a family man.

'How old is your son?' Bridget queried.

'He would be in his third cycle now,' answered Rufus. 'His name is Uriens; he was taken from me shortly after the queen's death, when he was still in need of a mother's milk.'

Bridget put a caring arm around Rufus and gave him a peck on his cheek. It put a warm smile onto his face.

'Fedel'ma is a very busy priestess and only sees those of authority. I could speak to her on your behalf, but it will not be until just before the new moon, several days away.'

'Ah well,' whispered Rufus, 'It was just an idea.'

'You could talk to Morr'igan,' Bridget suggested, 'She has a way to communicate with the spirit world. She can relay messages between her and the Goddess through the animal spirits.' Bridget noticed Rufus blush a little at the mention of Morr'igan's name.

'Is something going on between you two?' she asked, sitting upright in her chair, unsure whether to be alarmed or indifferent about the matter. Anyway, it was nothing to do with her. Rufus cleared his throat before answering,

'No, nothing is going on; we just watched the sun setting over the bay,' he lied.

'That's not what I heard,' came the voice of Lucifer from the corner of the room. 'Not according to Will, anyway,' the cat added, before once more drifting into sleep.

Rufus looked over to Lucifer in the shadows, curled up asleep on a chair, then across to Bridget who had settled back down into her chair again. He noticed a mischievous grin on her face before she saw him looking at her and regained her composure.

'Anyway,' continued Bridget, 'it is nothing to do with me, but I should add she has a sparkle in her eyes when she sees you.' Rufus began to blush again. 'I am sure Morr'igan will help you trace your son,' Bridget informed Rufus, 'Just be on your guard with her in matters of the flesh,' she continued, 'Her last lover, she turned him into a snake simply because they had a disagreement over something trivial.'

For a time, the couple sat in silence, listening to the occasional crack from the fire and the breathing of the pebbled beach, where

Rufus's men camped, as the waves crashed on the shore, moving the rounded stones up and down the beach. Rufus found it hypnotic and felt his body relax and his eyelids growing heavy. The peaceful purr from Lucifer in the corner added to Rufus's comfort.

In the unfamiliar world that surrounded Rufus a voice called out to him. He struggled to hear what the voice was saying. It was Bridget's voice, whispering into his mind, asking if he wished to visit the spirit world.

'Are you ready to go right now?' Bridget whispered. Rufus guessed he was ready and replied that he was. The faint smell of scent on the witch caught his senses as she held him close. His consciousness took him to a deep dark forest, with beams of light reaching down like spokes to penetrate the foreboding shadows. He was standing next to Bridget on a rough path that snaked its way through the darkness. They were holding hands and as happy as lovers.

ASTRAL ADVENTURE

'Where are we?' Rufus asked, looking around the dark forest. His heart was thumping in his chest and his breaths were short.

'You need to control your breathing,' Bridget said. 'I am your guide in my astral realm; close your eyes and relax, let your mind just observe. Take deep breaths.' Rufus concentrated on his breathing; i n h a l e ... h o l d ... e x h a l e ... h o l d ... i n h a l e ... Rufus could feel his body relaxing and his heart calming. H o l d ... e x h a l e ... h o l d ... The clutter of his mind was caught up in a refreshing breeze and carried away on the ether. I n h a l e ... h o l d ... e x h a l e ... Rufus felt calm and at peace, his mind open and eager for new experiences.

'Listen Rufus,' Bridget whispered, 'What can you hear?' At first Rufus could hear nothing, but as he listened, just concentrating on listening, he could pick up the sound of his breathing. Then he was aware of Bridget's breathing, in unison with his, in and out as one. Further away, the faint echoes of birdsong could clearly be heard drifting through the forest and the rustling of the leaves on the trees joined in the chorus of sounds that danced into Rufus's consciousness.

'What can you smell Rufus?' Bridget asked after a time. Rufus had a good sniff of the air, and the aroma of nature came flooding in, the earthy smell of the forest. Apples, Rufus could smell apples, and other fruit, and some exotic smells he had never come across before. One of the exotic aromas came from Bridget: a mixture of her scent and her natural body odour, the sweet smell entering Rufus's mind like a golden breeze of sea mist, obscuring the view of his inner world.

Bridget questioned Rufus again,

'What can you feel Rufus?' The golden mist dispersed, leaving Rufus's consciousness to gather at the outermost of his body. He felt where his clothes touched his skin and his hand in Bridget's, both generating a heat that spread to the rest of his body. Rufus could feel his hard leather boots protecting his feet and the firm track beneath him. A breeze of cool air caressed his face, making him smile. He felt a shimmer of vibration rise up through the earth, continuing up through his body, and causing small eruptions of bliss up his spine and out through the top of his head. Rufus's mind filled with a bright white light that blinded him, making him wince at its power. He felt Bridget's hand take a tighter grip on his and the light slowly faded, leaving his mind filled with the dark forest he was standing in.

'Now open your eyes Rufus,' Bridget instructed softly. Rufus opened his eyes to see that the forest was much lighter now or, at least, he could see much clearly now. The shadows were less dense, and he could see further into the trees. Blooms of every colour of the rainbow carpeted the forest floor and tiny woodland creatures and birds played amongst the trees and shrubs. The forest was alive.

'Come Rufus, let us walk,' Bridget instructed, pulling him with her as she stepped forward. 'If, for whatever reason, you want to return to the mundane world of matter just let go of my hand and you will be back in your chair around the fire.'

'So, this is not real?' queried Rufus.

'It is real,' answered Bridget, 'You can touch and feel things, connect with everything you see, and communicate with whoever you meet here. It is just a different reality, a different realm to what you know. Natural Laws are different here—nothing is born, and nothing dies; everything is, because that is how it is supposed to be.'

A butterfly swept past in front of Rufus, the breeze from the flapping wings caressing his face, bringing with it a sweet fragrance that only lasted a heartbeat before disappearing into the forest behind it. A movement in one of the sunbeams caught Rufus's attention and he pulled Bridget towards it. The light had caught the radiance of small faeries flying through it.

'Look at this,' called Rufus, as he studied the light beam penetrating the forest canopy. There were obviously hundreds of faeries hovering about the forest, but they could only be seen when they were in the light. One of the faeries noticed Rufus looking and stopped to converse with him.

'Hello man, nice to see you. Bridget does not often bring her friends here.'

'Err, hello fairy,' Rufus managed to utter back, a little shocked that this small creature had stopped to talk to him. He extended his hand into the ray of light introducing himself,

'My name is Rufus, King Rufus of Vindocladia.' The fairy cut him short by buzzing around his hand several times at speed, before settling down on the palm of his hand and resting against his fingers.

'Who you are is not significant,' informed the fairy, 'It is what motivates you that is important; your core belief is who you are.' What motivated Rufus? He was not sure, finding his son? The safety of his Kingdom, perhaps? The fight for justice, maybe? There were many things that motivated him.

'The core belief of everything is Love,' the fairy continued. 'Love is at the centre of everything; it is the energy that stirs the universe into action.'

Rufus pulled his hand out from the light and the fairy disappeared, reappearing again when he returned his hand into the sunbeam.

'My name is Eugenie,' the fairy told Rufus. 'I am an Elvin Wood Nymph, a guardian of the trees.' Before she could continue, another fairy came to hover over Rufus's hand to speak to Eugenie, something inaudible to human ears. 'I have to go,' Eugenie informed Rufus, as she took the hand of the second fairy and shot out of view in an instant. Rufus turned towards Bridget on his right, who stared back at him in delight.

'Come Rufus,' she smiled, 'there is something I would like to show you,' and she pulled him further down the path.

The fresh fragrance of nature swept through Rufus's senses as he and Bridget made their way through the forest. He felt a lightness in his step and a growing affection towards Bridget as they headed towards a small clearing, blossoming in light. Gentle music from the clearing drifted into his senses as they reached the radiance. An old, roofless ruin stood at the centre of the glow, with ghostly people playing woodwind and stringed instruments inside the tumbled walls.

'The Hall of the Great Ones,' announced Bridget, stopping at the edge of the clearing. 'They were the civilization that came before ours. They destroyed themselves with greed, power, and corruption.' Rufus looked at Bridget, surprised. He could not comprehend an earlier civilization than the one he existed in. 'We are the fourth civilisation,' Bridget continued, 'the other three are lost in the mists of time. Hopefully, ours will learn from their mistakes.' Rufus was so lost in the magic of the place he began to walk towards the ruin, nearly letting go of Bridget's hand. The witch gripped Rufus tight and stood firm. 'The inner sanctum is sacred to me,' Bridget revealed. 'I come here to learn of the old knowledge and wisdom of the universe and the future of the human race. It is my space and my space only.' Rufus returned to the side of Bridget, with lost civilisations seeping into his open mind.

'You can't go into her sacred sanctum, but I can,' sang Eugenie, the fairy. She had taken a liking to the King and had decided to accompany him on his journey. Rufus watched as the fairy, the size of his hand, flew into the ruin, whooping as she went. First, she sat on one of the crumbling walls, watching the musicians intently, and then she hopped up into the air and began to dance. So graceful the dance, the music began to follow in the wake of Eugenie as she skipped around the ruin of the Hall of the Great Ones. Then, as quickly and quietly as she had arrived, Eugenie disappeared into the shadows of the forest.

'Come,' Bridget ordered, and pulled Rufus away from the ruin. 'This is not what I wanted to show you,' she continued, as they left the clearing and continued along the path. Soon they came to a fork in the path, one path continued through the forest and the other led into a sunny expanse of undulating hills. Hundreds of round barrows that veiled the bodies of ancient warrior kings and queens thronged the tops of the varisized hills. A standing stone circle perched atop the closest hill to Rufus and Bridget, obscuring a large part of the view into the new bright reality and what lay beyond. Rufus wanted to climb the hill to explore the stone circle and get a better view of the barrow-filled land, but Bridget pulled him back.

'I can't,' the priestess shrieked, gripping Rufus's hand with determination. 'A dark force waits for me on the other side of the hill. I can't go in!'

Rufus looked at Bridget and was concerned at the fear she showed in her face.

'There is nothing to worry about; nothing will happen to you while I am here,' he boasted, then, as an afterthought, kissed her on her cheek. Bridget turned to face Rufus and held him tight in her free arm.

'I have tried many times to enter,' Bridget whispered, 'but always a dark energy looms from over the hill as I approach.'

Rufus looked at the top of the hill, the light grey stones calling to him. They had a message for him about Uriens.

'We have to go up,' Rufus instructed. Bridget pulled away and would have broken contact completely if Rufus had not had such a firm grip on her hand.

'No,' Bridget cried, 'Let go of my hand.'

Rufus held her hand tightly, allowing her to calm down a little before gently putting his hand on her cheek.

'Nothing will happen to you with me by your side,' he assured. 'I promise.'

Bridget stopped struggling and looked at the standing stones at the top of the hill. The dark cloud, unseen by Rufus, swirled above the stones like it always did, trying to suck her into its vortex, into a world of torture and pain. A world that was her memory of the not-so-distant past: that terrifying night when her husband, Mabon, was taken away by the Sea Dragon and the devastating scare that had stopped Drui'en from speaking a word ever since. Their world changed forever on that fateful night and Bridget knew she had to deal with that dark aspect of her past before she could move on. Today was not that day, even though she believed and trusted the man that stood beside her; what better time to face up to the darkness? Bridget looked at Rufus and smiled. She knew he would protect her, but she could not guarantee that she could protect him. Anyway, it was for her to deal with and her alone when she was ready.

'If you do not wish to go, then I will not force you,' assured Rufus, letting his grip on Bridget's hand loosen, allowing her to break free if she wished. She did not.

Bridget cradled Rufus's hand in hers and gave him a peck on the nose.

'Not today Rufus; anyway, this is not what I wanted to show you.' She led him along a small valley with the forest on their left and the hill following the path to the right. A small shaft of light penetrated the edge of the forest and the shadow of the hill, bathing the path ahead in light. Rufus watched as Eugenie appeared and disappeared, as she zig-zagged her way in front of them. Rufus was aware of the shadow that touched Bridget's presence from the hill but mostly she felt relaxed and carefree as they followed the path.

'Nearly there,' called Eugenie, as she accelerated forward and out of view.

'Nearly where?' Rufus called back but the fairy had gone.

'You'll see,' smiled Bridget, the dark energy having lost its power over her now they were close to their destination.

Bridget stopped Rufus and motioned him to close his eyes and listen. Rufus relaxed his breathing, allowing the outside world to meet with the inside world. At first, only the creatures in the forest called to his ears, then slowly he became aware of a constant hissing sound from ahead and tiny vibrations that danced beneath his feet.

'What is it?' asked Rufus.

'Keep your eyes closed and come,' answered Bridget and pulled the King towards the light. As they carried on forward, the hissing sound became louder, drowning out everything else. The ground shook harder, releasing its energy up through Rufus's feet and up through his body, resonating in his upper stomach. He could feel a cold mist envelope his exposed skin.

'This is the most beautiful sight in the universe,' Bridget shouted over the noise of the water cascading from across the abyss that stood in front of them. 'When I tell you to, open your eyes.' Rufus waited in anticipation for the wondrous sight that was going to invade his senses when Bridget screamed and let go of Rufus's hand. Suddenly they were both sat in their chairs around the fire in Bridget's home.

'What!' exclaimed Rufus, feeling the beauty of heaven being snatched away from him as he opened his eyes to a smoky room with Bridget holding her hands across her face.

'What happened?' Rufus yelled, more in shock than in anger.

'I'm sorry,' sobbed Bridget, 'I was attacked by a crow as I was about to reveal the secret garden to you. I panicked and let go of your hand. I'm sorry.'

Rufus leant over and gave Bridget a reassuring hug.

'That's ok,' he told her. 'Another time,' perhaps. Bridget looked up at Rufus,

'The crow that attacked me, I swear, belonged to Morr'igan. Are you and my friend lovers?'

'No, of course not,' replied the King, 'Why?' Bridget remained silent a while before answering.

'Just that she is trouble. Don't have anything to do with her; it will end badly for you.'

It was late and both were tired. Bridget gave the fire one last stir,

'I have a busy day tomorrow,' she declared, 'and I think you have a sentence to finish.' Rufus shrugged in resignation. He would worry about that tomorrow. He hoped that Eoaster had done what she had promised and hopefully ensured his freedom in exchange for his fearless deed. Now he was tired. The witch reminded Rufus to keep away from the potions' cupboard,

'There are some potions I make that you really would not want to sample,' grinned Bridget, as they hugged and kissed each other before retiring to their own rooms for a welcome visit to the land of dreams.

BATTLE STATIONS

The sun streamed in through Rufus's window, waking him up. As his brain began to relate to the world, he became aware of excited voices outside his room. While he dressed, he could discern the voices of two women, or possibly a woman and a girl. Must be Bridget and Drui'en, Rufus thought.

Had Eoaster made good her promise? What had become of the dirty Druid Balise?

Rufus found Bridget and her daughter hugging each other when he entered the main room. Both had tears cascading down their cheeks, tears of joy.

'Drui'en can speak,' Bridget cried when she saw Rufus. 'She has her voice back and she tells me it is down to you.' Rufus smiled at the happiness that the two women radiated.

'It was an honour to help you and your daughter,' beamed Rufus, as Bridget and Drui'en stood to include Rufus in their hug. For a moment, the three of them just stood there, hugging, and experiencing the joy that filled the room. Bridget was the first to speak.

Drui'en tells me that you went into the Underworld to help her; thank you.' Drui'en looked up to Rufus,

'Thank you,' she cried, still getting used to hearing her own voice.

'It was a pleasure,' Rufus replied, 'a real pleasure to help you both.'

Drui'en told Rufus and Bridget how a Goddess had come to her that night and taken her to a strange land. The Goddess called it a desert, an expanse of sand under a red-hot sun that threatened to cook them. Hung by his legs from a tree dangled the Druid Balise, sobbing and pleading for his life.

'Please, I am sorry,' the Druid whimpered, trying to look up from his awkward angle at Eoaster and Drui'en standing over him. 'Please forgive me Drui'en,' Balise pleaded to the girl.

'It is up to you what I do with him,' Eoaster told Drui'en, 'But if it was up to me, I would cut his balls off and feed them to birds.' Drui'en looked at the feeble man in front of her and felt pity for him. 'He has to be punished,' Eoaster stressed. Drui'en felt the dry, oppressive heat burn into her soul as she pondered what to do with the monster. He had abused her and hurt her and taken away her father and her voice. She wanted to see him dead but she had been brought up to show mercy and forgiveness. He had to be punished for the harm he had caused her and many of the other Portland children. Whatever she decided, the abuse had to stop. Eoaster interrupted Drui'en's thoughts,

'I can remove his sensibilities and turn him into a bumbling wreck; that way he is only dangerous to himself.' Drui'en thought about that. Balise would be no better than the crazies in the Infirmary at the Beale. He would be trapped in his own warped mind with his demons to torment him for eternity. She told the Goddess that was what she wanted.

Balise was found early that morning, in his hut mumbling to himself and eating his own shit—a terrible sight for the poor lad that discovered him when bringing his breakfast. The Archdruidess was informed and quietly the disgraced druid was delivered to the Infirmary before the sun had risen. It would not be long before Portland would know about his fall from power, which would come as a bit of a shock to most of the islanders. His demise was seen by the Archdruidess and others as a spell that had gone wrong, leaving Balise insane. It was seen by the druids as a bad omen that such an important man had been reduced to this. Shock echoed out around the island as the news filtered around the community, little knowing of the joy the news brought to a score of the children.

Two druid guards arrived, witnessing the three embraced souls through the open doorway. They, too, were in shock about the news of the old Druid of Justice and could not understand why Bridget, Drui'en, and Rufus appeared to be happy. Bridget noticed the two young druids watching them and broke off the hug to speak to them,

'Its Drui'en,' the priestess sobbed, 'she has her voice back. What can I do for you?' The two druids looked at each other before Agravain, the elder of the two, answered the witch.

'We have come to escort Rufus to the quarry.' The celebrations were brought to a halt. Rufus had forgotten that he still had to finish his sentence. Bridget would have none of it.

'You will do no such thing,' she argued with the druids, 'while he is in my care, he is my responsibility. You can tell the prison warden that Rufus had a relapse during the night and is in no position to quarry stone today.' The two druids looked at each other again, puzzled, as they were not expecting a refusal, especially when the man they had come to collect was standing before them looking fit to work. Before either of them could respond, Bridget took advantage of the situation,

'I said tell the warden Rufus will not be in today, so stop gawping and get going before I turn you both into frogs. I'm sure the warden would like to know before he arranges his work force for the day.' The druids took the hint: they had heard tales of people being turned into animals by the more powerful witches. Bridget had a bit of a reputation around the island that made them feel it was not worth the trouble of arguing and it was best to leave it for the warden to sort out. They still could not believe that Balise was now a resident of the Infirmary and unlikely ever to return. They bid Bridget farewell, turned, and walked as fast as they could back down towards the prison.

Bridget turned to Rufus,

'I will explain everything to the Archdruidess and have your sentence quashed,' she promised. 'It is going to be a beautiful day today; the sun is shining, and nature is about to spring into life. I want to celebrate by fixing up some food and drink and taking you and Drui'en to a special place that I know on the west cliffs.' That sounded like a good idea to Rufus and if he could, he would like to check in on his army before they left the island.

The view from the west cliffs was spectacular and reminded Rufus of his time with Morr'igan two sunsets earlier. Connecting the island to the mainland was the great pebble bank curving from the north of Portland to the west, creating the Fleet from Wick to Abbotesbyrig where it joined the mainland. A small but industrious village along the beach down under had spawned inland, up a steep hill that rose towards the hillfort perched at its top. From where they stood, Rufus could see his troops packing up and getting ready to leave. He was allowed to see them off, but first Bridget had a task to do and ushered him to follow her and Drui'en down a steep path that led down to the beach at the bottom of the cliffs.

The wind crashed into Rufus's face and the roar of the waves screamed into his ears. He could taste the salt in the sea air as he scrambled down the narrow path, not at all comfortable with heights, watching as Bridget and Drui'en effortlessly rambled down. Soon all three stood on the beach, a small cove only accessible from the steep cliffside path or the sea. Bridget pointed to a small crack in the cliff face and led him and Drui'en into it. After a few steps, the cave opened into a large chamber that was lit by a large aperture opening it to the above world. Spiral creatures of all sizes adorned the cavern wall and stalactites reached down from the roof. Bridget made her way to an altar lying against the inner wall and added cake and mead to the goddess icons and various pebbles. While Rufus looked around the chamber in awe, Bridget passed a piece of the cake around.

'I come here when I want to speak to the ancestors,' she told him, 'and to thank the gods and goddesses when it is due. I want to include you too in this today, with Drui'en, for releasing her from her enchantment. Eat.' Rufus ate the cake and drank the mead that was offered.

It was not a long ceremony but long enough for the gods and goddesses to acknowledge their blessings and the ancestors to be kept up to date. The remaining cake and mead were given as offerings and the cave became a little more sacred. Rufus felt warm inside and more relaxed than he had ever felt, but he wanted to let his troops know all was well before they left, and he wasn't looking forward to climbing up the path to the top of the cliffs. With luck, Bridget would be able to quash his sentence; he would see Percival was alright and then meet up with his men for the short march back to his castle in Vindocladia.

Rufus was gasping for breath by the time he reached the top; Bridget and Drui'en were waiting patiently for him.

'You don't get enough exercise,' Bridget teased Rufus, who slumped next to the women, causing Drui'en to laugh. Shouting made them look along the cliff at a man running towards them in alarm.

'Raibets, Raibets,' he was yelling to anyone who would listen. Bridget and Drui'en stiffened up and looked hard at Rufus.

'What is Raibets?' he enquired.

'Raibets are raiders from across the channel,' answered the worried witch. 'We must find the Archdruidess at once,' she continued, 'and prepare for battle.' The King, the witch, and her daughter hurried across the island to the hillfort where the druid army was gathering. The druid whose life Rufus had saved in the quarry, Dalan, saw them striding towards the fort and went out to meet them. He held out his hand to the King,

'First, I would like to thank you for your actions in the quarry,' shaking Rufus's hand vigorously, 'and second, I have the power to cancel the rest of your sentence. Under the circumstances you are free to go.' Dalan then turned to Bridget and Drui'en, 'A witches' council has been arranged in the great hall; you must hurry.' Rufus and Bridget looked at each other.

Was this goodbye?

It seemed all too quick. Rufus quickly made up his mind. He was not ready to leave. His army was nearby and itching for a fight. No, he would stay and help Portland against these Raibets. A messenger was sent to bring his men up to the hillfort, and Rufus joined the druids in the great temple to make plans while the invading boats of mercenaries and French wizards closed in on the island. A rough plan had already been hatched for an invasion, so the majority of the druids knew what they had to do. Druid Dobhran was in charge of the island defences and was already ordering teams into position around the cliffs. Dobhran faced Rufus,

'There are but 100 soldiers in your army,' he informed the King. 'The Raibets number at least 1000. It is not your fight; I cannot guarantee your safety.' Rufus shook his head at the commander,

'Ten to one is not bad odds,' he insisted, 'They do not know we are here, so we have the element of surprise on our side. I have a disciplined army at your disposal; it cannot be a coincidence we are here.'

'Look, there are 200 ships, each with about fifty pirates, closing in on our island right now,' roared Dobhran, 'and each ship contains a wizard, who is counteracting our magic that would usually repel the pirates. We can generally repel any sea attacks by calling on Taranis and the other storm gods to whip up the sea, but this time ...' The commander's word drifted into the wind. He knew he had a battle on his hands that he could quite easily lose, and the King's help would be useful.

Rufus put his hand on Dobhran's shoulder to reassure him,

'The pirates haven't reckoned on King Rufus and his army of expert fighters lying in wait; let them come!'

'Why not? Do what you can.' Dobhran concluded, giving Rufus a hug before returning to his officers who were still awaiting orders. At that moment, the witch's assembly came streaming out of the great hall, all waving their crystal staffs in the air. Around a hundred and fifty women, their cloaks waving in the sea wind, were preparing for battle alongside the druids. Rufus caught sight of Bridget, who was near to the front of the throng heading out of the gates, chanting, and calling on the war goddesses as they went. Morr'igan saw Rufus and left the warband to see him.

'Good luck,' he said, as they hugged.

'Good luck to you, my love,' replied Morr'igan. 'I heard you were staying to fight;

both me and Bridget admire your actions and hope to see you after the fight is won.' With that, the witch kissed Rufus on the cheek and left to join the last of the witches leaving the fort. Rufus was still unsure of how he felt about Morr'igan, or whether he could trust her, even.

Was she friend or foe? Was she playing with him or was her affection real?

Rufus was pulled out of his thoughts by a shout calling his name. It was General Griff at the head of his army, marching into the fort.

BATTLE OF PORTLAND

The view of the whole coast of Portland could be seen from the hillfort at the top of Verne's Hill. Rufus had Caliburn, his holly staff, which had been returned, and he was assessing the approaching pirate ships with General Griff. Most of the ships were heading towards Temple Cove below the shrine of Belisama, one of the few landing places onto the rocky island. The other ships were headed towards the natural port at Chiswell, below Verne's Hill to the northwest of the island. Rufus could see the port was protected by Portlanders stripped naked and painted in woad, preparing stacks of pebbles to use in their slings. They looked frightening and Rufus was glad he was on their side, but pebbles and slings would not be able to keep the pirates at bay for long; they would need help. Soon General Griff was leading thirty men down the hill towards the invasion shore. The rest of the army marched behind Rufus to Temple Cove.

    Rufus rested at the temple to give honour to the Goddess and to ask her to look after his men, and also Bridget and Drui'en. Morr'igan too for that matter. This was going to be a hard-fought battle for everyone on the island. Suddenly, a thunder bolt landed close by from one of the wizards. The druids responded with thunder bolts of their own; the battle had begun. Rufus could see that the landing cove the pirates were nearing was accessible only by a steep path that came up to the temple, and from there, the rest of the island was at their mercy.

'Ready for battle, Captain,' came a voice from behind Rufus. It was Percival, armed with a sword given to him by one of the druids. Stood next to him was a scrawny young druid who had been helping at the Infirmary with the hobgoblin.

'This is Merlin,' continued Percival, 'Despite his young age, he's very capable with magic and is willing to serve under King Rufus.'

'Glad to have you both by my side,' Rufus declared, watching the pirates attempting to negotiate the breakers before landing. 'There are some huge stone blocks on the edge of Wakeham village,' Rufus announced to the skinny druid, 'Do you think you could balance them in a line at the edge of the cliff here?'

'No problem, sir,' answered Merlin and within a heartbeat the stone boulders began to levitate themselves from the mason's yard down the valley to the cliff edge.

The pirates were now ashore and beaching their ships on the sand. Rufus and Percival watched as the invaders amassed and began to climb the steep path towards them.

'When I tell you to, Merlin, drop the stone over the edge,' Rufus ordered, before turning to his men and telling them to be ready. When the leading invaders were directly below the stone wall, Rufus turned to Merlin and nodded. Merlin raised his hands and gave a thunderous clap that saw the stones tumble over the cliff onto the charging pirates on the path. At that moment, Rufus charged his army down the path to meet them, screaming war mantras as they went. The pirates that were not killed or injured in the rock fall panicked and tried to return to the beach but found themselves trapped by the hordes behind them. With Caliburn spinning out in front, Rufus was the first to cut into the confused pirates and with Percival and his troops close behind, they were soon slashing and smashing their way through the enemy, quickly forcing them back onto the beach. The surprise attack had certainly done its job but now the remaining invaders had quickly reorganized themselves and stood solid, to face the outnumbered King and his army by at least seven to one. Suddenly more giant boulders came raining down on the pirates as Merlin sent more stone missiles into the ranks of the enemy. They shattered on impact, causing much blood and gore, and bringing down the odds to four to one. When the carnage was over, the King made another charge, forcing the pirates to scatter in all directions wondering what in Hades was going on.

At that moment, a thunder bolt from a wizard crashed onto the beach close to Rufus, causing him to fall backwards, hitting the ground hard, dropping Caliburn, and winding himself. He was lucky a swell had caused the ship to tilt just as the wizard was about to unleash his energy bolt at Rufus, or else he would be on his way to the Underworld again now. This time it would have been a one-way journey. Through unfocused eyes Rufus was aware of the grinning face of a pirate glaring down at him, with a giant axe raised above his head, ready to cut him in two. Rufus was helpless: half stunned, weapon less, and with his men too far away to help. He called on the Goddess to prepare the way for him to the realm of the dead, when a strange thing happened. The pirate was just about to bring the axe down on him when he suddenly stopped, dropped his war axe behind him, and fell to his knees. In front of Rufus, the pirate then turned into a squealing pig and made off through the battle along the beach. Rufus looked around and at first saw nothing that could explain this strange occurrence, but then he noticed a coven of witches on the southern cliff overlooking the cove, busy battling the invaders with their war goddess energy. Rufus saw Bridget among them, looking down to him, and giving him a short wave before continuing the battle to save Portland. The witches sent blazing energy bolts towards the enemy, who were racing back to their boats with the King's men in hot pursuit.

Of the 40 ships that had beached at the cove, only half that number escaped to the sea, leaving a good salvage in the possession of the Portlanders. The noise of the battle had been replaced with taunting and jeering from the Portlanders aimed at the retreating invaders, while the King's men rounded up the prisoners. The druids and witches were still exchanging thunder bolts with the wizards out at sea, but the ground battle had been fought off for now. There were still hundreds of pirates offshore, preparing for another attempt to invade.

A scream from the top of the cliffs drew Rufus's concentration away from the enemy, to see Drui'en trying to help as her mother fought for air. Bridget was on her hands and knees, struggling for breath. From where he was, there was nothing Rufus could do to help her. He scanned the cliffs to see who could help Bridget but saw everyone was engrossed in their own fight against the Raibets at sea. A small voice, barely audible above the crackle of energy flying overhead and the crashing of the waves on the cove, entered the mind of the King.

'Bridget is caught in the spell of a wizard further out than all the rest and out of reach of both druid and witch magic. Only you can save her.' It was Eugenie.

'What are you doing here?' gasped Rufus to the fairy he had met in the astral world.

'I'm saving Swan Feather,' Eugenie replied, 'Look to where I am showing you.'

Rufus could see the wizard that was attacking Bridget but what could he do? He was too far away to do anything.

'You have Fireblade,' Eugenie chirped into Rufus's left ear,

'Use your magic dagger.'

Was it possible Fireblade was the answer? The wizard was a long distance away. What was he to do? Throw it?

'Yes, throw it,' hurried Eugenie, 'It will find its mark; I will guide it to the wizard's heart.' Still Rufus hesitated.

'Fireblade will be lost,' he argued, doubtful that Eugenie's idea would even work.

'It is Fireblade or Bridget,' Eugenie declared. At that, Rufus knew that he had only one option. Fireblade was retrieved from the ether and, as hard as he could, he threw the dagger towards the target. True to Eugenie's word, Fireblade found the heart of the wizard, causing him to slump over the side of the ship and sink into the depths of the channel, taking the dagger with him. Turning towards Bridget, Rufus saw that she was breathing again and being comforted by Drui'en. He had done it; Rufus had saved her. 'And me,' called Eugenie, 'I helped too, you know.'

'Yes, thank you Eugenie,' acknowledged Rufus, 'I don't know what I would have done without you.' But the fairy had already disappeared back into her usual realm.

A shout echoed out from the top of the cliffs.

'Here they come again,' alerted one of the watching islanders, as 30 more pirate ships raced towards the small cove. The rocks from Merlin had stopped coming when the contents of the mason's yard were used up. Already the young druid was searching for more ammunition to fire at the advancing ships, but there was not much else to be seen.

'We shall fight them on the beach,' called Rufus, as he rallied together his troops. 'Let the Goddess be with you all. As soon as the bastards set foot on the beach, we slay them; they shall not make it up the cliff.' A great cheer of support came from the men. They knew today could be their last day on earth, but to die in battle alongside their King was an honour. Every man, druid, witch, and a hobgoblin were ready to fight and die when the first pirate ships crashed up the beach for the second time. Rufus and his men finished their prayers asking for strength and focus from their own individual gods and goddesses in the coming battle, when something large flying overhead caught their attention. Everyone looked up and were all staggered to see a dragon hovering over Portland. Nobody here had seen a real live dragon before. Most folk had heard tales of them, but dragons over the cycles had tended to keep away from mankind. The two did not mix. The gliding dragon had thick, blue scales covering its upper body, with a sea-green, soft underbelly. The force of its vast blue wings hit the battle scene like a storm, causing the ships still trying to land to collide into each other and capsizing some.

What now? thought Rufus, concentrating on the soft underbelly of the creature that had appeared, as if from nowhere, to involve itself in the battle. He was a little taken aback when the dragon appeared to only attack the pirates and wizards, overturning the ships, and ripping apart the pirates that had made it onto shore. Rufus and his men stood back and watched the carnage unfold in front of them, unable to really comprehend what was happening; it appeared as if the dragon was helping them!

From the top of the cliffs, the druids and witches stopped their magic when they first saw the dragon. It looked to them as if it had come from the cliffs and they too were amazed when it started to attack the pirates. What surprised them more than anything was the man that sat on the neck of the dragon, riding and controlling it. Who was this man? The dragon made short work of the invaders, leaving a small flotilla to escape back to France as a warning to others who might have intentions of coming to Portland. The waves lapped the shore around the cove, turning the shore red with the blood of the pirates. Seagulls flocked in to peck at the hundreds of dead bodies that were floating in the sea.

Rufus noticed that the dragon had landed somewhere at the top of the cliffs, and he was sure that he too had seen a man on its back. He ordered his men to round up any pirates still alive and bring them up to the top, before he rushed up the path to investigate the new arrival and check that Bridget and Drui'en were ok. At the top of the cliff, he found the dragon sitting quietly, licking its lips, while the dismounted rider pulled Bridget towards him and hugged her passionately. Rufus was a little stunned; who was this man? Drui'en saw Rufus and ran towards him.

'It's my dad,' she cried, 'he has come back.' Rufus's heart tightened a little, but he saw the joy in Drui'en's eyes and the love in her mother's embrace of the man from the dragon's back. Rufus turned to walk away and go back with his men; he did not want to spoil their moment.

'Please come and meet him,' Drui'en pleaded. Rufus thought for a moment, still getting used to the silence of victory. His body was still in battle mode, but his mind had drifted into a kind of numbness: the sort of numbness that comes from a loss. Drui'en asked Rufus again to come and meet her father.

'I would be honoured to meet your father,' Rufus informed Drui'en, putting his arm around her shoulder as they made their way towards her parents and the dragon. The dragon gave Rufus a snort of flame, stretched its wings, and let out a great roar when he approached its personal space. The King stopped dead in his tracks. Mabon turned to the dragon to settle her down.

'This is King Rufus,' Drui'en informed her father, 'and he saved us both from the enchantment.' Drui'en's father, Mabon, held out his hand to Rufus, who accepted it at once.

'Thank you, Rufus, I know what you did. I had a visit last night from the Goddess Eoaster, who freed me from my entrapment by Balise. It was Eoaster who convinced Henbane, the sea dragon who had been guarding me all this time, to return me home. When we arrived, we saw Portland was under attack. Henbane hates the people from across the channel for persecuting and killing all the dragons they found living in their lands. It was payback time for her.'

By this time, a crowd of druids had circled the dragon to pay her homage. The Archdruidess came forward to thank the dragon for her help in defeating the enemy. Henbane allowed the priestess of the druids to stroke her nose, before standing and letting out a great roar of flame to announce it was time to take her leave. The crowd stood back as the sea dragon gave a great flap of her wings and stared suspiciously at Rufus, before swooping off the cliff edge to glide above the sea for a while before disappearing into the haze of the noon sun.

The Archdruidess had some sad news for Rufus: two of his men had been killed down the bottom of the island, along with several islanders, when the pirates landed at Chiswell. That made seven of his men dead, including the five that fell on the cove beach alongside him. But she was pleased that the King's men fought well, both there, and here at Temple Cove. She would honour his fallen men with burial mounds on the western cliffs and would be privileged for him to build his castle overlooking the temple and cove. He would be the protector of the island, alongside the druids, witches, and slingers. Rufus liked the sound of that; over the past seven days and nights he had come to love Portland and its people, and he agreed at once.

Rufus remained on the island for several full moons to oversee the building of his castle, before returning home to Vindocladia. With the help of Merlin raising the stone blocks into position, the castle was finished in no time at all. A garrison of thirty of the King's men would be stationed at the fort at all times, to protect and keep safe the Portland community. Merlin spent a lot of time in the King's company during the building of the castle, listening to his many adventures. The young druid was inspired to leave his birthplace, to seek adventures of his own in the future. For his bravery and trust,

Rufus made Percival a warrior in his army. For all that he had done, Bridget made Rufus a member of her coven, who was welcome to any ritual they performed when he was on the island.

For now, Rufus would use the tranquillity of Portland to plan his next adventure. He was sure his baby son was being held in Brittany by his old adversary, Viviane, and he was sure Morr'igan knew something about it. He would have to get to know her better, despite Bridget's apprehension about her.

―――――

Rufus and Morr'igan spent a lot of time together while his castle was being built and became very close. Over time, he grew suspicious that she knew his son a little too well for a someone who claimed to be a stranger.

For now, though, Rufus would give her the benefit of the doubt and focus instead on a plan to rescue his heir from across the channel.

It would be a dangerous quest, but one that he knew he would have to attempt soon. However, for the moment, Rufus could relax and enjoy the pleasures that Portland offered.

The End

Printed in the UK
by
Clocbookprint.co.uk